TAKEN TO THE DEADLANDS

ELLE MAE

I just think fucking a demon who can barely control themselves so they have to wear a muzzles is hot, okay?

TAKEN
TO THE DEAD LANDS
A STOLEN DEMON BRIDE NOVELLA

ELLE MAE

NOTE

This is a work of fiction. Names, characters, business, events and incidents are the products of the author's imagination. Any resemblance to actual persons, living or dead, or actual events is purely coincidental.
Before moving forward, please note that the themes in this book can be dark and trigger some people. The themes can include but are not limited to; sexual assault mention, death, gore, nonconsensual biting, consensual biting, trafficking , eating humans ideation and mention, mutilation visuals, light animal abuse(throwing cat to the side).

If you need help, please reach out to the resources below.

National Suicide Prevention Lifeline
1-800-273-8255
https://suicidepreventionlifeline.org/

National Domestic Violence Hotline
1-800-799-7233
https://www.thehotline.org/

Also by Elle Mae

Blood Bound Series:

Contract Bound: A Lesbian Vampire Romance

Lost Clause

Winterfell Academy Series:

The Price of Silence: Winterfell Academy Book 1

The Price of Silence: Winterfell Academy Book 2

The Price of Silence: Winterfell Academy Book 3

The Price of Silence: Winterfell Academy Book 4

The Price Of Silence: Winterfell Academy Book 5

Short and Smutty:

The Sweetest Sacrifice: An Erotic Demon Romance

Eden Emory

The Ties That Bind Us

Don't Stop Me

Don't Leave Me

Don't Forget Me

Don't Hate Me

Hide N' Seek

Rate Race

Two of a Kind

TAKEN
TO THE DEAD LANDS
A STOLEN DEMON BRIDE NOVELLA

ELLE MAE

CHAPTER 1
MIA

Sometimes seeing ghosts had its perks.

As soon as the elderly lady hobbled out of my run-down shop, I started counting the massive wad of cash she had slipped me.

All I had given her were a few words of comfort. A tale or two of her deceased husband living it up in the afterlife. And a couple of far-off stares, and just like almost everyone that found their way into my shop, she believed it.

I had made a name for myself in the small town. The town of Fallhurst had only about two thousand people and had only grown a few handfuls in the five years I'd been here.

I was poor when I arrived—still was if I was being honest—and had no way of making money. But it only took me a few days to realize the small quirks of this town.

This town loved the supernatural.

And with this money, I have enough for monthly rent on this shop, and I can even afford a treat for myself.

A part of me felt bad for taking advantage of some of these people in their grief-filled states, but money was money.

A high-pitched whine drew me from my thoughts.

I looked back to my desk where my cat, Momo, sat looking at me with her big green eyes. Also a customer favorite. She would often sit on the laps of customers as I went about my show, soaking up all the attention and warmth. One could almost think she was the perfect accomplice. Putting everyone at ease while I worked my magic.

I bounded toward her, letting my hand run across her smooth, black fur. She leaned into my pets, her purr filling the quiet shop.

"Maybe I can get you a treat too," I whispered to her.

When she looked up at me and meowed as if understanding my words, I couldn't help but smile.

"For an ex-stray, you sure are spoiled."

Not that I minded. I would spoil that cat with everything I had. After all, she was all I had besides this shop.

I had been lucky to find her one day behind my dumpster. At the time, she was all skin and bones and hadn't gotten her nails trimmed in what looked like years. When I took her to the vet, they rushed her into emergency medical care.

She fought to survive, and after that, there was no way I would have been able to leave her behind.

The doorbell chimed behind me, causing my heart to speed up.

Another customer? Maybe my luck is finally kicking in!

I turned to greet them but jolted back when I instantly came face-to-face with a person—*no, not a person.* I gripped the desk behind me with all my might for fear that I might faint if I didn't.

She could have been confused for a person if it weren't for the bright red horns jutting from her forehead. They poked out of shiny white hair and circled backwards and out. Dark black veins trailed from them, running down her forehead and sticking out against her pale skin.

Wide red eyes filled my vision, looking at me with a playful expression. What should have been the whites of her eyes were completely black.

I couldn't speak, couldn't move. Fear had taken hold of my entire body.

"Spirit seer," she breathed. Her voice was husky and held a bit of a growl to it. "It's been a while since I've seen one of your kind."

I opened my mouth to speak, but no words came out. She tilted her head to the side and took a step back. Only then did I notice two things.

One, she had brilliant red wings sprouting out of her back. They were so large, the tips of them brushed the ceiling of my shop.

Two, she had barely any clothes on. She was covered in a red, shiny, spiderweb-like material that covered her breasts, parts of her stomach, pussy, and legs, starting mid-thigh.

"Can you not speak?" she asked. "You were just talking to the old lady? Maybe I should get her—"

She turned back to the entrance, and whatever panic had been holding me back now forced the words out of me.

I might have been a scammer, but I wasn't about to put that lady's life in danger.

"Wait! I just—what the fuck are you?"

She turned to me, her black-painted lips turning into a wild smile. Her clawed hands came up to rub her chin.

"Isn't it obvious?" she cooed. In a flash, she was in front of me again, invading my personal space. Her hands spread across the desk behind me, and I had to lean back so our lips wouldn't touch. "Guess for me, spirit seer."

I swallowed thickly. Her entire demeanor was playful, but something eerie radiated from her and had dread taking root in my stomach.

It was like she was dangerous but trying to play... innocent?

What the fuck is happening? Am I really playing a game with some sort of monster?

"You look too evil to be from heaven," I murmured. "From hell?"

Her smile was so wide, it was like it split her face in half.

"A spirit seer should know that it's called the Demon Realm now."

I couldn't help the huff that forced itself from my lips.

"Well, *excuse me.*"

She leaned back with a laugh. I quickly thought about grabbing whatever was left on my desk and hitting her over the head with it, but her eyes were back on me in milliseconds.

"The others will like you," she said through her laugh. "A bit of an attitude is always fun in the beginning."

In the beginning? What about the end? What is she going to do? Beat it out of me?

Not that's a terrifying thought.

As she turned to look at the entrance, my gaze shot toward the back. There was another entrance there, but I had boxes of shit piled up in front of it. A total code violation, one I was now regretting. But if I could make a run for it—

Clawed hands grabbed my hair and yanked my head back.

"Not so fast," she threatened. "Can't have the goods running off so soon, can we? Your *buyer* may like a bit of a chase, but I don't."

Ice cold fear filled my veins.

The fight-or-flight response kicked in, and I pushed her back as hard as I could. To my surprise, she actually stumbled. Maybe someone of her power wasn't expecting their prey to fight back, but no matter. I would take it.

I used her stumble to my advantage, crawling over the desk, and bolting straight for the back door. All the papers, pens, and cups were flung across the floor. My heart felt like it was going to burst in my chest and blood rushed through my ears.

Faster. Go.

I stumbled, falling to the floor, but managed to push myself up and made a break for it.

I skidded to a halt when the shrill sound of Momo's pained screams hit my ear.

My head whipped back to see the demon with Momo in her claws. She had her dangling by the scruff on the back of her neck. Momo was giving a hell of a fight, but the demon didn't even blink. Not even when Momo sank her claws into her forearm.

"Run and I eat her."

All my hair stood on end.

Run. My mind begged me. *Run. Live. Forget the fucking cat.*

I gritted my teeth.

What? Now you want to be a good person?

I hated that I was being weak.

I didn't struggle all those years or fight like hell to make my place here, just to have it blow up in my face because I couldn't leave the goddamn stray I had picked up.

But regardless of what my mind was telling me, I couldn't run. Not when the sounds she was making caused my heart to crumble and not when it felt like she was *begging* for me to save her.

Each moment I paused, the louder her screams got.

"Give her to me," I ordered.

The demon gave me a look.

"You won't need her where you're going."

She held out a hand for me. Going against every survival instinct I had, I walked toward her but didn't place my hand in hers. She clicked her tongue and threw the cat to the side.

I snapped my head in her direction just in time to see Momo land on her feet. The demon took the chance to grab me.

It was useless to fight her off this time.

As soon as her hands were on me, light burst forward from her chest, and the entire world fell around us.

CHAPTER 2
MIA

One would expect to wake up with a headache when they are kidnapped by a demon, but when I opened my eyes next time, it was quite the opposite.

It was almost as if I was being pulled from the best sleep of my life. My body felt light, and there was a thrum of heat spreading throughout my limbs.

With a sigh, I turned over, trying to grab the fluffy blankets around me and pull them closer.

Just a few more minutes... When was the last time I had slept this well?

That's when the whispers broke through the thick haze of my still sleep-ridden mind.

"It's been too long. Maybe we should wake her?"

"The longer she sleeps, the better."

"But maybe we can think of a way to escap—"

There was a rustling not far from me.

"You know that's not an option," a girl hissed. "Just let her be blissfully unaware of our situation. I'd join her if I could."

"What if they come—"

I groaned as I pushed myself up. Their voices had begun to buzz around my head like two incessant flies.

"I'm awake, Jesus H. Chri—"

I lost my train of thought when I pried my eyes open to look at the girls.

Both were sitting on a bed that had been placed right next to mine and dressed in the same outfit. A thin slip that covered nothing.

My bed was high off the ground and decked out in furs and comfortable-looking pillows. From what I could see, the same was true for theirs.

No wonder I felt so cozy.

My gaze darted around the room as images of my encounter with the demon filled my mind.

Kidnapped. I was kidnapped.

Or at least that's what I thought, but looking at the room I was in, it looked more like a place for royalty than prisoners.

The walls showed exposed brick, but they were draped in beautiful, glittering tapestries. The floors were covered in rugs of a similar material. Above our heads was a large chandelier that reflected light onto everything around us.

"Are you okay?"

I looked at the girls in front of me. The one I assumed had spoken looked at me from under her thick lashes. Her skin flushed the longer I stared. Her eyes were a brilliant shade of purple I had never seen before. That, combined with her fair skin and white hair, made her look ethereal.

"I'm... as good as I could be after getting kidnapped."

The girl next to her threw her head back with a loud laugh.

Her hair was dyed a deep blue that caught the light as she moved. When she moved to wipe the fake tears from her eyes, I was met with an amused stare. Her brown eyes took me in with obvious interest, and she leaned back onto the bed with a small smirk.

"At least your brain's working," she said, then nudged the girl next to her. "This is Iris. I'm Eve. There are a few other girls, but it's been a while since we've seen them. I assume they're dead."

"*Eve!*"

I gave Iris a forced smile when her panicked eyes caught mine. They roamed over my frame before she visibly relaxed.

"I'm Mia, by the way."

Iris gave me a nod before turning to glare at Eve.

"We don't know what happened to them, but you shouldn't scare her," Iris muttered.

I didn't know how long they had been cooped up here together, but they seemed to be particularly close. So much so that a bit of envy wormed its way under my skin.

"Can't you tell if she is or not?" Eve asked.

"I'm not that good of an actor," I answered her question myself with a small laugh. "I'm still trying to digest everything, so I'm not sure my mind knows how to be anything but confused right now."

Eve sat up straight, giving me a devilish smile.

"No, that's her thing," she explained. "She can *see* it, can't you, little mouse?"

"Don't call me that." Iris visibly puffed at her nickname.

I couldn't tell if their casual attitude was helping or hurting in this situation. I gripped the bedding, trying desperately to calm my racing mind.

All of this was too much, too fast, yet I still needed answers. Ones I wasn't sure they were willing to give.

"See what?" I asked, desperation seeping into my voice. "Please. I'm losing it here."

"I can read emotions," Iris said after a moment. "*See* them. Kinda like an aura."

I swallowed thickly. "So, what can you... see?"

Eve looked at her as well. Iris shifted her eyes, looking down at her hands.

"You're confused. It's frustrating you. You weren't scared... until I told you about my gift. Sorry."

Panic rose in me.

"It's not you. It's just this whole situation—"

"It's okay, I was freaked out about it too," Eve said. "I don't like people seeing into me like that. Which brings me to you. What can you do? Read minds? Fly? Teleport?"

I gave her a look.

"What do you mean?"

She rolled her eyes.

"It took a lot of talking, but we figured it out between us and the few that came before you," she offered. "We all have something. Iris is auras. I can tell when someone lies. And you?"

I stilled. The two girls in front of me looked normal. Like any other humans walking the earth.

What do they mean they have special powers? And why do they think I have—

No.

Realization, closely followed by horror, hit me like a truck.

Seeing ghosts was a lie!

The townspeople believed it, but... That demon? Was that the reason she kidnapped me in the first place?

I'm going to throw up.

"She's having a breakdown."

"*No.*" My voice came out harder than I meant it. "It's just... She called me a spirit seer."

I looked up sheepishly. Both of them looked at me with varying degrees of hesitancy. I prayed to whatever power was out there that Eve wouldn't catch me in my lie.

Because it wasn't *technically* a lie. The demon did call me that... But whether that was true or not was a whole different story.

I'm obviously much worse of an actor than I thought.

Eve relaxed a bit. "Well, then maybe you can spot the one that comes into our room to deliver food."

Iris didn't say anything, but she wouldn't look me in the eyes either.

Can she tell? Even worse... Will she tell Eve?

"Food?" I asked. "How long have you been here?"

"Almost a week," Eve said. "Iris is on day three."

Without warning, the door burst open. I jerked back and pushed myself to my knees, eyes trained on the door.

"Oh, it's the food," Eve commented. "Don't try to run. That's how the last one disappeared."

I had been lying the entire time. I had not once seen a ghost. But the thing that walked through that door?

It was the most twisted, grotesque thing I had ever seen in my life.

Whatever it was, it wasn't a ghost. I had nothing to compare it to, but my gut feeling told me that thing was far worse than any spirit.

Its body was skeletal-like, with skin that looked more like leather than anything human. Chains were wrapped around its body, and low moaning sounds came from its disfigured mouth.

It didn't look our way as it set the plates down on the floor, nor when it turned to leave. The door shut behind it automatically.

"So... did you see it?"

I swallowed thickly and looked back to the other two.

"That wasn't a ghost," I murmured. "Whatever it was..." I shuddered, unable to finish my sentence.

"It's angry and in pain," Iris whispered. "Maybe another type of demon?"

Eve shook her head. "If that was the case, we would see it."

I wanted to tell them that there was no way that was a ghost either because I couldn't see ghosts, but I kept my mouth shut.

I'm not sure what the demon wanted with us, but I knew that if I wanted a chance at surviving this, I needed to play my cards right.

CHAPTER 3

ARIS

I loathed the auctions.

I hated the smell of lingering fear and arousal. I hated having to interact with the demons that were invited. And most importantly, I hated seeing the demons tear apart humans without a second thought.

It had been almost a millennium since I stopped feasting on humans. Since the fear they exuded left a scar on my psyche. Since I had lost control.

Back then, I had been a young demon, looking to regain the power to protect what I cared about. But when that was taken from me, the pain of going through these auctions never seemed worth it.

"Aris, what the hell are you doing here?" a grating, yet familiar voice called.

I stiffened in my seat. I had made sure to get the one closest to the back and in the shadows somewhat, just so no one would come up to me.

Apparently, they didn't get the message.

I gritted my teeth and looked at the intruder—or *intruders*.

Two twin girls stood off to the side. One stood tall, with her hands shoved in her suit pants. Her button-up was loose, and on top of it she wore a suit jacket with an embroidered royal coat of arms.

Her twin looped her arm around her neck, her chin on her shoulder, and looked at me with a devilish smirk. Both had a messy type of mullet that was dyed a light reddish pink. Or at least I thought it was dyed, since no member of the royal family had that monstrosity of a hair color.

Maybe it's bloodstained. That would be more on brand for them.

Small, delicately filed horns peeked from beneath their hair. Another sign of their heritage. Demons like myself and many others didn't have the resources or even bothered to constantly file their horns. But for royalty, it was a must.

Everything about them had to be groomed for presentation to the inner courts—from their clothes to what they ate to even the women they fucked.

How they got away with half of what they did was beyond me.

Last I saw them, they were being taken in for punishment after poisoning the royal family's food supply. Anyone else would have been beheaded for even *attempting* to kill a royal. These two, however, succeeded in killing three of their relatives before being caught.

But even as demons gathered from across the realms to see their punishment... They walked out to greet us without so much as a hair out of place.

Even I had found myself a little impressed with how they managed to pull that off.

Against my inner wants, I stood and bowed my head to them.

"Eros, Oros."

"Oh, knock it off, Aris," Eros said. She was the one in front and usually the one that did the talking. Oros, on the other hand... Let's just say she liked to play more than she liked to talk. If Oros was talking, trouble was expected.

I gave her a forced smile.

"I, too, am bound by the rules, Eros," I replied. "No matter how long we've known each other."

Oros turned around and motioned for the human worker to get them chairs. The man seemed to be young, maybe in his twenties, and while he looked well fed, the terror of witnessing this auction had left his cheeks hollow and eyes dead.

I sat down with them when their seats were brought over.

"Answer the question," Oros demanded as soon as she sat down.

I took a deep breath. *Answer what you need to. Give nothing else.*

"I heard there was a spirit seer here," I admitted.

Oros let out a laugh that was so loud, it caused others to turn and stare at us. I cursed her for her lack of tact.

"And what would *you* need with a spirit seer, hm?"

"To eat them, of course," I quipped. "Maybe steal their power if I am able to."

It was mostly a lie. Demons could rarely steal a human's powers after devouring them. It was nothing more than a myth because no demon would ever actually admit to having stolen the powers for fear that they too would be eaten.

"Didn't you stop eating humans?" Eros asked. My eyes narrowed on the darkened stage. I didn't want to meet her calculating stare. She would see right through me.

"What about you?" I asked, deflecting.

Eros let out a hum.

"There is a human lie detector here," she said. "You and I both know how well that would do in court."

I nodded. Demons were notorious liars, but the royal family even more so. They were cunning, ruthless, and I did not envy Eros and Oros's life.

"Maybe we can have a bit of fun with them as well," Oros whispered, her excitement obvious in her tone. "According to Beau, their nectar tastes just as sweet as their blood."

My hair stood on end, and an unrecognizable heat flared in my belly. How many years had it been since I had a chance to taste a human that way?

Memories of her body against mine. Of her sounds as she came. All of it hit me so hard, it felt as if I'd seen her yesterday as opposed to a millennium ago.

"Aris."

Fuck. Can I just be left alone?

"Yien," I greeted, looking off to the side. I might have banished myself to the shadows, but Yien was born from them. She could have been standing in the corner the entire time, and the darkness would have hidden her presence. I wouldn't have put it past her. She stepped forward, the shadows melting away as soon as she stepped into the dim light.

Her inky hair fell to her waist in straight, silky strands. Her light purple horns jutted out from her head and curled backwards. Looking closely, I noticed the dark jewels embedded in them. Her all-black eyes narrowed on me, the ghost of her white pupil the only thing that let me know I was her target.

Unlike the others here, myself included, Yien didn't dress up for the occasion. Instead, she wore a loose robe that tied around her waist and pants that hid most of her frame. They, too, were all black. I didn't have to look down at her feet to know that she wasn't wearing shoes.

She never did.

"I need your help."

I bristled at her comment.

Help? Since when am I the one to ask for help?

"You want one?" I asked.

She gave me a stiff nod. It wasn't hard to read her. She might have been just as old as me, but sometimes she acted more like a child than the terrifying demon she was supposed to be.

"I have enough money for one or two rounds, but not more."

"Too bad they don't take that god-awful glitter that falls out of your ass," Oros commented.

Yien's eyes narrowed toward the twins. I let out a sigh.

Yien and I were as close as I was with the twins. Meaning not at all. But unlike the twins' massive pile of cash, Yien lived in the Shadow Realm, where the need for money was nonexistent. They lived off their powers and rarely came to auctions like these unless they were desperate.

"Why do you need a human all of a sudden?" I asked.

Yien's eyes looked back down at me. I couldn't glean any information from her expression. Maybe that was a good thing. I feared for the day that she showed *actual* emotion.

"I want a companion."

Oros let out a laugh that caused a few of the demons in the room to look over at us once more.

It angered me. I didn't like that the demon was being made fun of. I too knew what it was like to be chained up in a realm with no warmth but my own.

"If you want a companion so badly, just fetch one of those demons your estate employs. I'm sure they'd jump at the chance to get a mouth full of—"

"Once you run out of money, let me know," I found myself saying. My better judgment was telling me to stay out of it, but I couldn't help but feel for the demon.

"Thank you," Yien whispered and took a step back into the shadows. She didn't cover herself fully, just enough for us to still be able to see her face and clawed hands. It would be enough for me to know when to take over.

Damn, between Yien and myself, just how much money am I going to drop today?

It wasn't every day the four of us showed up in one place. To bet on humans, no less.

The crowd roared to life when lights flooded the stage. A small, winged demon with brilliant white hair and red horns took center stage.

No one knew her name. We all just called her Madam. She had been in charge of this auction house for as long as I could remember, and she specialized in bringing the tastiest humans to the Demon Realm.

"Who's ready to purchase some humans?" she asked, a wicked smile spreading across her face, showing off all her sharp teeth.

Here we go. I will buy the human. Take her home.

And when all is said and done, I will finally be able to move on from the hellish life I have been living.

CHAPTER 4

MIA

They forced us out of our beds and dragged us away, kicking and screaming, in the middle of the night.

Or at least I thought it was the middle of the night. Not that our cage had any sunlight or windows to prove it. And as nice as it was, there was no denying that it was anything other than a prison. Though, if you asked me, I could have probably spent a few more days there without complaint.

The demons that barged in to get us were all wearing the same black uniform, and many of them looked human, save for the horns, claws, and sharp teeth. At least it wasn't that creepy fucked-up thing from before.

Iris allowed them to take her without much fight, giving up almost as soon as her feet touched the hallway outside our room.

Eve and I, on the other hand...

"Get your hands off me, you fucker!"

I tried to break out of the guards' hold, but both of them were quickly on me, forcing my arms to my side. One of them was already fed up with my screaming and forced a hand over my mouth. I tried to bite it, but the skin was so hard it probably hurt me more than it hurt them.

At least Eve was giving them hell. She screamed, kicked, and slapped them. Too wild of an animal for them to contain.

It wasn't much use though. We were still dragged down the dark hallway and into an even darker room, where we were pushed to the ground. As soon as the demons' hands were off me, I pushed myself up and tried to get to the door before they closed it, but some kind of force knocked me down.

Glowing rope-like objects circled my upper body before pulling tight, constricting my movements. I turned back to look at the culprit but was met with another demon guard. By the looks of his glowing eyes and glower, I assumed he oversaw the others.

They were brutes, but at least they couldn't shoot glowing magic at us.

"Be gentle," he warned the other demons that surrounded us. "Humans are fragile, and the buyers will be really upset if their goods are damaged."

Buyers? Goods?

I shot the other girls a panicked look, but both of them already seemed to be frozen in place, gaping at the demon.

I guess we all heard the same thing.

Hands gripped me and forced me up once more. This time, I couldn't find it in me to fight them.

"It's not like they would care anyway," one of the demons by my side muttered.

"Right?" said the one that held Eve, looking back at us. "They'll be too busy in a feeding frenzy to notice a bruise or two."

Fear clogged my throat.

The demon in charge huffed as we passed him.

"Remember that not every demon is here to get a human to feast on," he reminded them. "Some come to find a companion or someone to bear their children. Either way, they pay good money..."

His voice trailed off as the incessant thoughts in my mind grew louder.

What? No.

Run. Fight them. Do something.

I turned my head to look back, but there were guards following us from behind, and with my arms currently bound, I wouldn't be able to fight them like I needed to.

Eve flung her whole body back. The demons on either side of her scrambled to hold her, not expecting her to react so suddenly. At the same time, my guards' grasp on me loosened just slightly as the ones in front stumbled back.

I took my chance.

But instead of darting backward, I darted forward.

The only guards in front of us were already trying to keep their humans under control, so I guessed they wouldn't try to grab me.

And I was right.

I slipped beneath Eve's legs, dodging the hands that failed to take hold of me.

"Go Mia!"

Iris, who had been compliant until now, clashed against her guards, throwing them off balance enough for me to slip past them.

When I pushed back the curtains that separated us from the next room, bright lights blinded me, but I couldn't stop. Not when I could feel the demons right behind me.

Loud rumblings and cheers called my attention. I blinked a few times until my eyes adjusted and followed the noise.

I froze for just a moment, taking in the darkness of the room in front of me. I realized in that moment that I was on a small stage and people—*no, demons*—were all around. I couldn't distinguish their faces because of the lights, but I could make out distinct shapes like horns, sharp glittering teeth, glowing eyes, and the heavy feeling of death in the air.

I didn't let it shock me for too long and kept moving across the stage until I ran into a hard chest and it sent me sprawling. The demon reached for me, and I screamed and jerked against his hold. When he tried to cover my mouth with his claws, I bit down hard on his hand. His loud growl roared in my ears.

In an instant, his weight disappeared, only to be replaced with another. I turned my head to see the demon fighting two others that had to pull him to the other side of the stage. His eyes were wide and bright red, his teeth bared, and loud growls rumbled from his chest.

"Oh my, it's your first appearance, and you've already caused a frenzy," someone said from behind me.

Dread hit me hard as I was pulled to my feet only to come face-to-face with the demon who had whisked me here in the first place.

I opened my mouth to scream at her, but with a single wave of her hand, my throat felt like it was on fire. A cough racked my body, and my lungs burned. I couldn't breathe.

She didn't stop whatever magic she was doing until black clouded my vision and another demon held me up. I tried to fight him, but his hand was wrapped around me and gripped my face, forcing me to watch the crowd. The longer I stared, the more I could make out the horrific faces that looked back at me.

Some of them could pass for humans, but many looked like something straight out of my nightmares.

"Since the spirit seer offered herself up so prettily, we shall start with her," my kidnapper said from the side. "Spirit seers are rumored to have a sharp taste, with hints of winter and mulberry. We will start the bidding at three thousand royal gold, though remember you can always offer something from your realm to *sweeten* the deal."

The volume of the room raised in response. I couldn't make out the bids, but the white-haired demon seemed to have no such problem.

"Five thousand gold and... a mermaid scale! Okay, anyone... Six thousand and a dragon egg? No, no, that would raise it to at least ten thousand gold. Can anyone match?"

The noise around me quieted as my heart slowed.

Is this it? Is this really how it's going to end? Am I really being auctioned off to fucking demons in another dimension?

I didn't know how long the bidding went on, only that the entire time I was faced with the cold, hard fact that there was absolutely nothing I could do to save myself.

"Eighty thousand and a soul sphere going once... twice... Sold to Demis from the Fire Fields!"

My breath caught in my throat. There were a few grumbles here and there, but overall, the commotion quieted.

A large demon who was at least seven feet tall walked up to the stage. His entire body looked rock-hard with wound like slashes all along his limbs and face, showing a burning red color underneath. He stood tall, though his back seemed to be hunched permanently. His mouth opened to show me a set of decaying but sharp teeth.

"Touch me and I'll kill you," I forced out, but it only made the demon laugh.

"Come, human, it's been years since I feasted—"

His eyes widened and his entire body froze. A smaller figure stepped out from behind him, her eyes narrowed in on me.

She was unlike any other demon I had seen before. Her skin was gray with an iridescent shine to it in the light. Her long black hair fell to her waist with two long strands braided back, keeping most of it out of her face. Two deep blue horns jutted from her head and curled back.

She wore a loose blue silk robe that was open in the front, showing off her bare chest, and loose black pants that were tied at the waist. Her claws were tipped in black, and only then did I realize that one of them was also dripping bright red blood.

She let out a sigh and pushed the giant demon away, causing him to tumble to the stage. No one attempted to catch him as he rolled off it.

"Seventy thousand." Her voice was low and husky and caused a thrill to go through me.

I looked at the white-haired demon to my right. There was a small smile on her face.

"Killing the bidders is against the rules," she tutted, though she didn't seem all that angry.

The demon girl shrugged.

"We know you won't punish me, so why don't you just give her to me?"

The auctioneer demon cocked her head.

"It's been a while since you've had a human, Aris of the Deadlands. Pray tell, what amuses you so much about this one?"

Aris. That was her name.

Aris shrugged.

"Take it or leave it," she grumbled. "No one can match me."

"Eros and Oros can."

Aris's mouth twisted into a snarl.

"They will not bid on this one. Give her to me. I am running out of patience."

The other demon sighed but didn't fight her.

"Seventy thousand going once... twice... Sold to Aris of the Deadlands!"

When Aris's gaze met mine, my breath was stolen from my chest.

This woman—demon—is going to eat me.

Another thought followed that one.

Well, at least she's hot.

ARIS

This little human is going to fucking ruin everything.

Not only had she burst out headfirst onto the stage, but even as I brought her back to my spot to sit, she fought against me.

"Let me go, you asshole!"

She tried to pull her tiny wrists from my hand, but she was too weak, like most of her kind. Still, I pulled her to me, needing her to come close. When she winced, a shot of guilt burst through me.

"Just be good," I warned, leaning closer to whisper in her ear.

The weight of the eyes of the many demons in the room made my skin burn. It wouldn't be good for me if they saw my weakness. It wasn't uncommon for demons to take a human companion, but not many treated them with respect.

Nor did they let them throw a fit in the middle of an auction.

Madam's voice sounded behind me, and the auction was resumed.

The human looked back to the stage, and I took advantage of the distraction to pull her away.

She didn't fight me as hard this time. Maybe because we were headed straight to the twins and to the people who were already focused on bidding on the next human.

"A royal favor." Eros's voice wasn't loud, but it carried far, silencing anyone who so much as attempted to speak over her.

Even the human knew not to say anything as I sat her down in my chair. She attempted to make herself smaller by folding her shoulders in and putting her hands between her legs. I knew the right thing to do would be to kneel in front of her and calmly talk her through this, but I had an image to uphold.

I felt Yien come to my side before I saw or heard her. The coldness of her shadows enveloped us and caused the human to look up at me with a startled expression.

I was met with hazel eyes with long, damp lashes. Umber skin shone under the dim lighting, enough for me to catch a glimpse of the dark freckles that lined her face and neck. Her brown hair was stuck to her skin, which I now realized was slick with sweat.

The human is scared.

"Cover us more," I ordered Yien.

"My human is next."

"This won't take long."

Yien's shadows filled the space around us. I dropped to my knees in front of the human, and she straightened suddenly, giving me a grim expression.

"I don't taste good," she said quickly. "I have a human blood disease that is slowly rotting me from the inside. If you're not careful, I'm pretty sure you can catch it too."

For the first time in years, a smile threatened to tug at my lips.

I leaned forward, close enough for my nose to brush across her chest. Her heart was beating so fast it drowned out all sounds around me.

I inhaled deeply.

Pain stabbed deep at my gut. My throat constricted. Drool pooled in my mouth. My teeth ached.

I jerked my head back, not trusting myself to get any closer.

The frenzy was already playing at the corners of my mind, reminding me of how long it had been since I feasted. Memories of my sharp teeth tearing at human flesh, of the taste of their blood bursting across my tastebuds, of their magic filling my veins hit me like a truck.

I closed my eyes.

"I won't eat you," I forced through clenched teeth. It had an edge to it that I hoped wouldn't scare the human. "I have other plans for you."

Another scent hit me. One I wasn't too sure I had enough control to assess.

This time, I shot up to my feet and exited Yien's shadows.

I hadn't heard the commotion, but as soon as I was away from the human, my senses flooded back.

Demons were growling and yelling all around us. Chairs were being thrown. Bodies clashed against bodies.

"Empaths are a hot commodity, it seems," Madam called out over the roaring crowd. "Let's add something interesting to this bet, hm? Does anyone have another soul sphere to offer?"

Yien raised her hand. Panic burst through me.

I don't have what she's offering.

"Put your hand down right fucking now. You do not have a—"

"I do," she said, her tone not giving any indication of her lie. "A soul sphere for the human. No royal coin."

Madam threw her head back with a loud, crazed laugh.

"Don't kid yourself," she spat. "Anyone else—"

"A soul sphere... of a realm ruler."

Silence fell across the room.

It's not possible. Demons didn't have a soul to capture, so how—?

"Proof," Madam demanded as the human on the stage shook with fear, her eyes wide as she watched us.

Yien gave her a quick nod before looking over the crowd. When her eyes fell to the already dead Demis, a slow smile spread across her face. She didn't move from where she stood. All she did was send her shadows over.

All-black tendrils shot out from her shadows and circled Demis's large body. With ease, they held him up, and we all watched as the shadows attacked him, moving over his skin as if searching for something. Then they started pulsing. With each pulse, the body they covered got smaller and smaller until—

"How is that possible?" I breathed. "He was dead."

The shadows dissipated until there was only a single, black orb with a red core floating where the body had been.

Quicker than I could have thought possible, I turned around and yanked the human out of Yien's shadows.

Yien's eyes cut toward me.

"That hurts me," she deadpanned. "I thought we were friends."

"I didn't know you could—"

"Sold!"

Yien's gaze snapped back to the stage, and, in a flurry of shadows, both she and the human were gone.

I paused, looking at the twins, but the spot they had occupied was already empty.

A tug on my arm caused me to look back down at my human. Her eyes were wide, and the anger from before seemed nowhere to be found.

"Mia," she said. "My name is Mia."

I gave her a hard look.

"You want something... *else*, right?" she asked. "If so, you should at least know my name. After all, I do know yours, *Aris*."

My name falling from those lips shouldn't have set me alight like it did. Neither should her scent.

So, what the fuck kind of human are you, Mia?

CHAPTER 6

MIA

I was going to get fucked by a demon.

A demon with large horns, clawed hands, and sharp teeth.

Why does the thought of those same clawed hands gripping my thighs cause my cunt to clench like this?

Still, I ignored what my body was telling me.

I would fuck her, but only because I was sure it was the only way I would live through this. And after, once her guard was down, I would find a way back to earth and—

All the thoughts in my mind came to a complete halt when I came face-to-face with the... monstrosity the demon called a home.

I thought the long walk through the creepy, misty woods had been bad... but this?

Maybe if the stone was not cracking, or the windows broken, or the grass wilted, or the dirt blackened, the manor could have looked hospitable.

It was large and towered over us. In a period drama, I would say that the same type of house would look regal, but having it plucked from a bright, cheerful setting and dropped here to rot for god knows how many years caused it to look… horrific.

"The Deadlands, huh?" I commented, looking toward the demon.

Her lips dipped and her brows pulled together. It was the most expressive I had seen her be—if I could call it that—since she leaned forward and sniffed my chest. Her eyes had returned to normal. The dark veins that lined her face were gone. And now she looked at me with something akin to annoyance.

"Your aptitude is astounding," she muttered. "It is like it's named. Dead. Everything, everywhere."

I swallowed thickly.

"Can a human survive here?" I asked.

She gave me a quick nod and motioned for me to follow her. This time, she didn't try to pull me along. *I could try to make a run for it.* But she didn't seem too worried about it.

Maybe it's because she knew I wouldn't be able to survive in these lands without her.

So I followed her.

We walked up the hollow-sounding steps, and she pushed the door open with ease.

"Water, electricity, warmth, food, servants. I have prepared everything."

Even though the inside was still basked in dark grays and blacks, it was almost… cozy. The light was dim, and the main entrance opened into a foyer where there was a large staircase that led up to what were probably other wings. Decorative dark rugs were strewn about, and frames covered the walls, though none of them had any portraits.

I caught sight of another demon off to the side.

She was dressed similarly to Aris, though her robe was much less extravagant. It was black and somewhat plain. Her white hair and black horns were in stark contrast to each other. Black veins lined her forehead, and her nostrils flared. Her eyes slowly started to turn red.

"Leave." Aris's voice caused me to jump.

The demon bowed and turned back toward the right side of the house, disappearing into what I assumed was another living space or even a dining area, though I couldn't be sure because of the lighting.

Aris's gentle hand glided across my back. Only then did I realize how warm it was in the house. Her action only caused heat to fill me even more.

"Will she eat me?" I asked.

"No one here will touch you," she vowed.

I nodded shakily. After what happened in the auction house, I had no reason to doubt her ability, but somehow living in a demon realm with demons I had no idea would be able to control themselves enough not to eat me left me feeling less than secure.

"You sure know a lot about humans, huh?"

Her hand left my back so quickly I had to turn to make sure it wasn't yanked away.

"All demons do," she said, though her tone had turned hard. "Let's get you to your room, and we can discuss what I need from you."

What she needs from me. My stomach flipped and heat rushed through me.

I had a moment to take her in, and it was hard not to notice how lean and well-built her body seemed under those robes. Monstrous or not, I was attracted to her.

So, hopefully, this will be enjoyable for the both of us.

Even though my instincts told me it would be more than just that.

I couldn't speak as she led me to the wide staircase and to the second floor. The hallways were filled with open-doored rooms, but when I peeked in, not one soul was lingering.

We stopped at a closed door, and she pushed it open, giving me a look into the biggest room I had ever laid eyes on. It was even bigger than the shitty apartment I had above the shop.

The entire first room had large, albeit cracked, windows. A bed that could easily fit three people.

Or maybe a human and large clawed demon.

There was a seating area off to the side and two doors to the right, which I guessed led to the bathroom and closet. Oddly enough, there was a bookshelf to the left filled with old, battered books. From my position, I couldn't tell if they were in English.

"So, what do you... need from me?" I asked, trying to swallow the knot in my throat.

"Sit down." She motioned toward the bed. "You must be weak from everything."

I rolled my shoulders and moved to sit on the bed with my hands in my lap. I didn't know why I expected her to do something as human as sit beside me, but she moved to stand in front of me instead.

Sitting down, I had to strain my neck to look up at her. She said nothing for what seemed like a long time.

What is she going to do to me? How is this going to happen?

"I had a human before," she finally said softly.

So, she knows how this works. It makes sense that the entire place was "ready" for a human then.

I nodded, and with a shaky hand, I reached out to grab her clawed one. She jerked away at first, but after a moment, she relaxed and let me take it.

"I didn't want to come here," I admitted, though I didn't know why. "I still want to go home. Even if it's the shittiest place I've ever lived."

Maybe I thought it would force her to take pity on me. Or go easy on me, so to speak.

She surprised me by squeezing my hand lightly.

"I'll take you home after you help me."

Hope burst in my chest. I searched her face for any indication that she might be lying, but there was none.

That's it? So, what, we fuck, and I get to go home?

The idea of fucking a demon shouldn't turn me on as much as it did, but still, a low heat filled my belly, and my heart rate picked up.

It could happen any second now. It had to happen any second now. We were in the perfect place for it. I mean, there was even a bed.

Though I'd be lying if I said that the thought of her pushing me against the wall to ravish me wasn't appealing.

"That easy?" I asked, my voice rising.

She gave me a stuff nod. "That easy."

I stood up. She was so close, our chests were brushing against each other.

With shaky hands, I pushed off the straps of my slip dress. When I let it fall to the floor, her nostrils flared.

"What are you doing?" she asked, her voice deepening. The veins were back, and she bared her teeth at me. Red played at the sides of her eyes, but didn't overtake them fully.

I should recoil, but instead, I slowly wrapped my arms around her shoulders.

"What you paid for," I answered. "You had a human before, so you know how to handle me, right?"

"This is—"

I leaned close enough for our lips to touch. I wanted to kiss her. Even if she had teeth as sharp as knives.

"Be careful," I whispered. "Or your expensive toy will break."

Without another word, I pressed my lips against hers. For a few awkward moments, she just stood there, frozen against me, but then her clawed hands gripped my waist.

Then, as if something switched inside her, she began kissing me back. Forcing her tongue between my lips and exploring my mouth in a way that gave me no time to react.

I whined and pushed myself against her, but it wasn't enough.

Her hands cupped my ass before trailing to my thighs and lifting me before I wrapped my legs around her waist, shamelessly grinding against her in search of friction.

She pushed us to the bed, her hand coming up to grasp my throat. When she pulled away, my breath caught. She looked just like she did in the auction house. Red eyes. Face overtaken by those veins.

But there was a hunger that hadn't been there before. One that made her look like she wanted to devour me... in a *different* way.

"You smell like you want me," she growled, her eyes trailing down my body. Her hands pushed open my legs, exposing me to her.

I couldn't stop the shiver.

"And if I do?"

Her eyes shot to mine.

"Is this the payment you require?" she asked. I raised a brow at her and opened my mouth to speak, but her clawed fingers coming to rub my clit caused all thoughts to disappear from my mind.

The claws were so sharp I worried for a moment that they may hurt, but it was overshadowed by my lust for her. I may have even welcomed the bit of pain as it mixed with the pleasure.

"Payment?" I managed to croak out somehow.

"For what I require of you," she reminded me. "You want your payment to be in orgasms?"

I let out a low moan when her fingers trailed down my folds and to my entrance. They were teasing, careful not to add too much pressure.

It only made me wetter. She was pacing herself. A demon who could murder me in the blink of an eye was trying to control herself instead of just taking me.

"Orgasms are a given for what you require."

She nodded.

"I can't taste too much for risk of frenzy, but if we're careful…"

I was going to ask what the "frenzy" was, but then I forgot all about it. She pushed a single finger inside me, and her claws didn't nick me. Instead, all I felt was a blunt fingertip.

Not enough.

I reached out to her, but she shook her head.

"I'll stay here," she said. "To be safe."

There was something vulnerable in the space between us. In me being completely naked while she was still fully clothed. In me writhing and moaning at only the touch of one finger while she was just standing there, still as stone.

"Please," I murmured, spreading my legs even wider for her. "*More.*"

CHAPTER 7

ARIS

er scent attacked me. Her blood, her sweat, the smell of her delicious cunt. Everything swirled around me, goading the frenzy.

I never once imagined that the human would feel this way about me. To actually *want* me to touch her. Though I would pay just about anything for her power.

But I would be lying if I wasn't excited about this chain of events. Lying if I said I wasn't insanely turned on by the human naked in front of me.

Her moans only pushed me forward. I wanted to hear more of them. Wanted to know what she sounded like when she came.

And more importantly, I wanted to hear what my name sounded like when she was moaning it from those beautiful lips.

It had been so long since I was able to touch a human like this. Since I had *wanted* to touch a human like this. After *her*, I never thought I would feel like this again. It was confusing me.

With one finger still inside her, I trailed my hand from her throat down to her chest, then pushed on it hard enough to keep her immobilized.

Stay in control.

It was easy to imagine sinking my claws into her chest and tearing her heart out. I let out a growl and forced another finger inside her instead. Her cunt was already gripping the life out of me. I curled my fingers inside her and used my thumb to rub her clit.

My darkest desire was to make this last for as long as the human could take it. To see just how much she would be able to take before she fell apart. But I couldn't let myself get that distracted. Couldn't let myself enjoy this as much as I wanted to.

I applied more pressure to her sensitive bundle of nerves. The faster she came, the faster I would be able to reel myself in.

She arched into my hand, and I watched her perfectly erect nipples just begging to be sucked.

My mouth watered, and before I knew it, I was leaning forward to take the dusty brown peak. Her pussy clenched around my fingers, and I used it as the sign to pick up the pace of my thrusts.

"Fuck, don't stop," she moaned.

When I fit a third finger into her, she let go of all inhibitions. She bucked against my hand, her moans bouncing off the walls.

And for the first time in years, I felt a dull, pulsing heat between my legs.

It was so sweet. The smell of her. The taste. It had the frenzy getting closer and closer by the second.

Before I could stop myself, I lightly bit her nipple. She tensed, the pain throwing her into her orgasm. She cried out, arching her back. The movement was abrupt enough it had my teeth ripping her soft flesh.

The sweet taste of her blood flooded my mouth, overtaking everything. Every thought of wanting to fuck her was replaced with something else. Something more violent.

My body jerked back before the frenzy could take hold of my mind.

Stupid. Stupid, horny demon.

I pushed away from her and slapped my hand over my mouth and nose. If I wasn't careful, even just breathing her scent would cause the frenzy to worsen.

And even though I knew that, I still let myself lick the lingering blood from my teeth, unable to conceal the moan of tasting delicious human blood for the first time in forever.

I wanted more. Like an addict, I was already itching to take an even bigger bite next time.

I caught sight of her sitting up on the bed with a dazed expression before I turned toward the exit. All rational thought had left my mind, and I was only filled with the need to feast. To go back and *take*.

My legs were the only ones that listened to my wishes. They stayed still, binding me to the ground.

Images of going back to the bed, sinking my teeth into her, all while fucking her until she couldn't even remember her own name flashed through my mind. I would make it good for her, that much I knew.

She wouldn't even know what hit her. She wouldn't scream and cry. No, she would be begging me to keep going.

But after? After, she would end up just like *her*.

"Are you—"

My head snapped to look at her. I hadn't heard her approach, but when I turned, she was a mere couple of feet away from me. Still naked and with her arm reaching out to me.

She has a fucking death wish.

"Don't!"

She flinched as the gargled sound of my voice ripped through the quiet of the room.

My eyes narrowed on her bloodied breast. I hadn't realized how deep I had cut her. And still my mouth watered.

I took a shaky step toward her.

"Sorry," I said after clearing my throat. "Let me help you clean it up. I'll be gentle, I promise."

My voice had changed. It was soft, enticing. The frenzy was still there, but instead of openly attacking her, it was trying to coerce her into letting me devour her. I was falling further into it without even realizing.

The frenzy wouldn't attack her openly at first. It would try and coax her into giving in. Make her give herself to me willingly. Only then would I lose all control and it would be too late for her.

Her arms crossed over her chest, and she turned to the side. She was shaking.

"Go calm yourself," she whispered. "I will clean up. Please don't come back until you are ready. I don't want to di—" She paused before continuing. "We have a deal, don't we? I'm no use to you if I'm... dead."

Her words cleared enough of the haze for me to force my body to turn around and march straight out of that room.

CHAPTER 8

MIA

I didn't even have time to bask in my orgasm before my situation all but literally slapped me in the face.

Two hours had passed since Aris left me alone in my room. I had been forced to clean up the wound on my tit, grimacing when I realized just how bad it could have turned out if she hadn't pulled away when she did.

I had been so turned on by her being so in control—or so I thought—that I forgot she could actually kill me without so much as a warning.

The closet had been stocked full of clothes that looked and smelled clean. Mostly robes like hers, many of which had splashes of pink and intricate embroidery on them.

There were a few pairs of pants here and there, and even panties that looked pretty and brand new.

The entire room seemed to be in much better shape than the rest of the house.

Meaning she had been waiting for me.

Or for any other human was my next thought.

But I didn't want to go there.

The bathroom was also stocked, and I had access to hot water. The only downside was how freezing it was in the room. So, even though I wasn't the slightest bit tired, I was forced to curl up in bed for warmth.

I hadn't expected her to come back, but then there was a small knock on the door, so faint I almost missed it.

"Come in."

There was a pause on the other side before Aris pushed open the door. She looked much better now. The veins were gone, and she even looked ashamed. Her hair was damp and stuck to her skin along with her clothes.

After what happened, I should have been scared. Or at least turned off by her.

But my eyes still followed the stray droplets that flowed down her chest.

During our time together, I had caught sight of grayish nipples that had stood erect under those robes and that were now peeking through the soft fabric. My mouth watered at the memory.

"Is now an okay time to talk about what I require?" she asked.

I frowned. Seriously? No *Sorry I almost ate you* apology?

"Sure. Just... keep your distance."

She nodded and closed the door behind her without making a move to come any closer.

I sighed and beckoned her. She hesitated but crossed the room, stopping in the middle.

"I didn't mean to lose myself like that," she offered. "So, after you hear my terms, I would like you to pick a different payment."

I raised my brow at her.

"So it was my orgasm that caused you to lose control?" I asked.

She tilted her head to the side.

"No, the blood."

Confusion blossomed inside me.

"Then just don't bite me next time?" I suggested.

She huffed and shook her head.

"Even just touching you like that spurs on my frenzy," she confessed. "Your smell, the feeling of you around me—all of it makes me want to... *taste* you. And you seemed to like it last time."

Her words caused heat to flood my face. I wasn't normally a bashful girl, but god, that sounded dirty coming from her mouth. I expected her to remain unaffected, which seemed to be mostly on par for her except for when she bit me, but her eyes got a faraway look in them, and she ended her sentence breathlessly.

So sex would be... difficult.

"Then how are you going to require me to have sex with you if you can't handle it?" I asked, nervousness filling me.

She paused, allowing silence to fall over us.

"I don't *require* sex from you, human." She spat it out like she was offended I even mentioned it to begin with.

My blood froze. *Wait, she doesn't? Then... why?*

I shot up, pushing the blankets off me.

"Why did you let me jump you like that then?!" I all but shrieked. She cringed at my volume, her lips twisting into a grimace.

"*You* were the one who said it was your payment for helping me."

I opened my mouth to speak, but no words came out. Humiliation burned at my face.

I realized why she hesitated then. I started taking off my clothes before she had even finished telling me what she wanted. I was the one who came on to her.

Jesus Christ, Mia. How fucking horny are you?

"So then... Why did you buy me?"

She let out a heavy sigh and placed her hands on her hips, looking down at the floor, as if trying to decide whether the task of explaining herself was worth it.

When her eyes met mine again, my heart stopped in my chest.

"Because you see ghosts, and I need to contact someone. The... *human* who was here before you."

I sat back on the bed and forced my mouth shut.

So many thoughts were running through my mind and at a million miles per second, but it really came down to one thing.

I just jumped a demon without knowing what she wanted from me, and now I have to tell her I can't see ghosts.

She would throw me out. Or worse, really eat me this time.

"That's it?" I asked, my voice rising an octave. "You just need to make contact, then I can... go home?"

She gave me a stiff nod.

"I planned to pay you for your work while you were here, but I underestimated how I would react to touching a human again."

Again. Touching a human... again.

"Oh no," I whispered, rubbing my hand over my face. "And this human... You were... together?"

And for some reason the idea of her with this other human was bother me.

When she didn't answer, I snuck a peek up at her, but she wasn't looking at me. Instead, her gaze was fixed on the window.

"I bought her like I did you," she explained. "But back then I had been looking for a companion. And well..." She shook her head as if trying to force the thoughts out. "I need you to contact her ghost. I'm hoping it's still here."

I didn't know what to think. I was left with the feeling that I had fucked up horribly. That she had been desperate to get me to contact her ex... lover? Human pet? And I had thrown myself at her, thinking she wanted to fuck me.

"I—I didn't realize."

She sighed and looked back toward the exit.

"This was her room when she was here," she explained. "I was hoping you could sense her. I'm not sure how your gift works."

I wanted to throw up. Here I was, invading her previous partner's space, even trying to fuck her in this same room. Everything was falling apart.

"What... um... happened to her?" I asked.

Aris stiffened. "You don't need to know that. Just tell me what you want."

I shook my head.

"Just let me go when we are done," I said. "That's all I need from you."

She nodded wordlessly.

"But it would be easier if you told me more about her," I added after a moment.

Somewhere, far off, a clock chimed.

"Later," she said with a look that caught me off guard. I didn't know what I expected from a demon, but it wasn't the emotions that were twisting up her face. "Sleep well. I'll wake you in the morning."

CHAPTER 9

ARIS

Would she fear me if she knew?

No, she already did. I could smell it on her. Even if only a little bit.

The real question was... Would she still be willing to help me if she knew?

It wasn't that hard to believe that, once she knew the horror her fellow humans had suffered at my hands, she too would come to resent me for the being I was.

At least we would have that in common.

I had tried my best over the years to keep a human-free diet, but it was against everything us demons had been taught growing up. And went completely against my instincts.

But still, I would keep trying. For her and the others who came before her.

And she had yet to pick a price for her services.

There might have been demons in the Underworld that treated humans with little respect, but I wasn't one of them. At least not anymore.

She was here to help, and she should be taken care of as such.

I looked down at the human beside me with a small frown. *Mia.*

She hadn't eaten much at breakfast, and now she was at my side, staring up at a decapitated statue that had been a favorite of my last human.

"So, what is this?" Mia asked, her voice sounding a bit... bored even.

I shot her a look.

"Humans don't like this?"

She shrugged then looked up at me with an almost forced smile. "Art, you mean? I guess, but it looks like you had a bone to pick with this one."

Her words caused my lips to twitch. I was surprised she picked up on it. The other human had just assumed it was meant to look like that.

I had expected Mia to say something about yesterday, but this morning she had yet to mention what happened. Embarrassment and humiliation burned my entire body all night, causing me to get the worst sleep of my entire existence.

I was the one who procured this deal, yet I was also the one still having trouble asking her for what I truly needed. Maybe it was the pain of remembering what had happened, how her blood had tasted on my tongue, and how I had felt when my teeth ripped through her flesh. Or maybe it was the moans and cries that still haunted my mind, along with my name falling from her lips.

"Oh my god," she said with a light laugh. "Got mad and chopped its head straight off, didn't you?"

"I wasn't mad," I answered with a frown. "I was upset."

"What could a demon from hell be upset about?" she asked.

"My meal running away," I admitted, my eyes shifting to her. Her smile dropped for a moment before she forced it back onto her face.

"So, is that why we're out here? For you to remind me who's in charge here?"

I shook my head. "I heard that soul pieces can reside in places humans used to visit."

Her eyes trailed my face.

"You're not wrong," she said after a moment. "Though it would be strongest where she died. Unless this place was really important to her, I doubt her ghost would be wandering around here."

"You didn't hear anything last night?" I asked.

She shook her head and crossed her arms over her chest.

"Not gonna lie. After being kidnapped and sold to a demon, the last thing that was on my mind was looking for a ghost. Exhaustion caught up to me, and I was out like a light," she replied, and I nodded.

"Let's try again soon then. When you're ready, I'll accompany you to your room."

She pulled her bottom lip into her mouth, her teeth grazing it softly. I didn't want to admit what that action did to me.

"I guess we'll have to wait and see if she stops by for a visit," she said, her voice trailing.

I shifted on my feet, unable to stand the guilt gnawing at me, but I couldn't pinpoint its origin. Did I feel guilty because of the vicious murder I had committed or because of what I was about to spill to Mia?

"If anything, her soul would have remained there because I killed her there," I blurted out, watching her expression intently. She was good at hiding her fear, but I could smell it on her.

Her eyes widened just a fraction before they went back to normal. Her teeth dug into her bottom lip a bit too harshly, and the smell of sweat filled the air, just like last night and at the auction. The frenzy was in the back of my mind, begging me for just a taste.

But then as fast as it came, it was gone. Like she was trying to... mask her fear. My heart swelled. *Perfect little human.*

"You killed your companion," she said. I nodded.

I thought long and hard last night about admitting it, but after tossing and turning, I thought it might be the best-case scenario. Maybe if I told her the truth, it would help her connect faster. And the faster she connected, the faster I could tell her what I needed, and then the faster Mia could leave this place.

"Why would you kill your companion?" she asked, her voice dropping to a whisper.

I tore my eyes away from her and back to the headless statue.

"I didn't mean to."

My voice cracked, the emotion that filled it embarrassing for a demon. We shouldn't feel anything for our human playthings. We shouldn't feel bad for them. We shouldn't think twice about eating them. Yet here I was, upset over what happened lifetimes ago.

"Back then, I still ate humans sometimes," I admitted. "And when I was with her one night, much like what happened between us, she started bleeding. Normally, a small amount shouldn't faze me, but I hadn't eaten in a while because she didn't like it and I wanted to—"

I couldn't finish my sentence.

Mia didn't push me to.

I jumped when I felt the warmth of her hand in mine.

"Let's take this slow. We can begin whenever you feel comfortable."

CHAPTER 10

MIA

I pushed through the dead tree line, the branches that had fallen to the ground crunching under my feet.

My breath stopped in my throat when I spotted Aris just a few feet away, right near the edge of the cliff. It was already hard to breathe because of the short hike, but when I saw her there, it felt like I had the weight of the world on my chest.

I hadn't seen Aris after our interaction near the statue the previous day. Food was left outside my bedroom, and I kept staring at the door, just waiting for her to stop by.

But she never did.

I was conflicted. Half of me wanted her to come by, half feared she would.

I paced. Read some of the books that she placed in the room. Many of which were actually English classics that I had heard or read about growing up.

The beaten up spines made me wonder just how many humans had ran their fingers down the peeling spines before I had.

I hadn't asked her to finish her story before. I hadn't had the heart to. It was all I could think about.

But seeing her here, looking out beyond the cliff with such a saddened expression... It caused my chest to ache.

Whatever that human had been to her, there had to be so much more than the little hints she was dropping. The pain etched onto her face was something I had only seen in my most grief-ridden clients.

She turned to look back at me, and in that moment, the pained expression on her face was gone. She almost looked... at peace.

"I used to like it out here," she said and motioned for me to come forward.

I followed her lead, but because she was so close to the edge, I also reached out to grab her hand. The action caused her eyes to widen.

"Sorry," I muttered under my breath. "I'm scared of heights."

A small smile spread across her face.

"We won't get that close," she promised. "And even if we did end up falling, it wouldn't kill us. I wouldn't let it."

I gave her a look and peeked over the edge. Below us were miles and miles of dead trees. When I squinted to see beyond the mist, I could make out barren lakes and even the dash of a few wild animals, though I was afraid of what type they might be.

All in all, if it wasn't so desolate, it might have been a beautiful view. Forests as far as the eye could see. Probably even some flowers below, adding pops of color to the area.

"I can see why you used to like it here," I said with an appreciative nod.

"Really?"

The astonishment in her voice caused me to look at her. Her grip on my hand became tight, and I wasn't too sure she was aware that she was doing it. Or just how much her face had lit up.

"Really," I replied with a small smile of my own. "It's beautiful, hauntingly so. In the Human Realm, we have many places like this, but the trees would be green and there would be grass or flowers below."

She gave me a quick, enthusiastic nod. "I have seen them. Forests the likes this realm has never seen before. I was in awe the first time I saw them."

I raised a brow at her.

"You have been to the Human Realm?"

Her smile dropped at this.

"I haven't always bought humans in the auctions," she explained, though her voice was hesitant. "It's expensive, and there was a time when this realm had a portal, but it has long since disappeared."

"A portal?" I asked. "Is that how you travel? Can you make one?"

She shook her head. "That is not the power I possess." She lifted our connected hands and showed me as she changed her claws to fingers. "Like manipulation, though it's hard to sustain."

No wonder she fingered me like she did.

"To hunt. You visited to hunt humans."

"Yes," she admitted. "Though I did try to find a companion once or twice before *her*. I brought them here as well."

Maybe I should have felt afraid knowing I was just another human she brought here, but I couldn't. Her intentions seemed good.

Afraid? Not really. Annoyed? Oh yes.

Better not to think about it, though.

I nodded and looked back at the land below. It really was something out of a horror movie. But I wasn't lying when I said I liked it. It was beautiful. But in the same way Aris was beautiful. Otherworldly.

"If you see there..." Aris pointed out to the far right. It took me a few seconds to figure out what she was pointing at, but I gasped when I saw it.

"More demons?" I asked. I could just barely make out their hunched forms in a large dip in the ground. There were about ten of them, and they seemed to be digging something up.

"I employ them. To dig up the roots of the dead trees. We sell it to make alcohol and potions for witches. Some demons swear they can get high off it."

I gave her an astonished look.

"So *that's* how you have so much money."

If I didn't know any better, I would say the slight darkening of her cheeks was a blush.

"It pays well," she confessed after clearing her throat.

"I bet," I said with a light huff. "And them? I didn't think anyone lived here besides that one demon girl."

"They live far on the edges of my realm with their families. I allow them free rein of the area as long as they work to dig up the roots."

"That's nice of you." I leaned back to get a better look at her. She just shrugged. When her eyes looked back out at the forest, they turned sad. "When was the last time you came here?"

"A long time ago," she sighed. "I liked to show this to the humans. Like you said, I thought it would remind them of the forests of their homes, but..."

I didn't like how the words came harsher at the end. Lead filled my stomach.

"Did they try to jump? Is that how you know it won't kill us?" I forced out, trying to not make my words sound as hollow as they felt.

Her silence told me what I needed to know.

"It's okay to talk about them," I said, squeezing her hand.

"You don't feel... disgusted?" she asked.

"Sometimes scared," I admitted. Her face fell. "Sometimes upset. But... You are a demon. And given what I saw, eating humans is in your nature. So, I can't really fault you for trying to survive."

"And the companions, what about them?" she pushed.

I bit my tongue before answering that one.

"I'm guessing they all came here unwillingly?" A nod. "Did you... force them to—"

"Never," she spat. "I would never. Companion doesn't always mean sex. Sometimes I just wanted a friend. A partner. I employ demons, but we don't make friends often. They usually live alone, save for their mates. I just wanted..."

I felt like pushing a bit more. But this time she surprised me by taking a deep breath and continuing.

"After a while, I would offer them passage home. I learned to do that after the first one slit her wrist in front of me to provoke me into a frenzy," she explained.

"How many?" I asked.

"Three. The second one didn't make it through the portal before it collapsed. In her anguish, she fought me and I—you can guess what happened."

I nodded.

It should be horrifying. I should be disgusted. But instead, it made me feel things I shouldn't. I just sent her a small smile.

"It's okay," I said. "It's hard, I know, but don't give yourself over to guilt. I can see it messes with you."

The hope in her eyes was almost enough to break me.

What the fuck am I doing, telling her it's okay to lose control and attack humans?

But a part of me understood her struggles and recognized just how much she was trying to change.

Even if thinking that way could be my downfall.

CHAPTER 11
ARIS

"It looks… very appetizing," Mia said with an obvious grimace. Sarcasm was heavy in her tone.

My smile fell, and the pride that had ballooned in my chest deflated.

The past couple days, I had taken food to her room for fear of her being around Thera. This was the first time I had Mia eat in the formal dining room on the first floor. I decided to mark the occasion by helping Thera prepare some of the human delicacies I had learned from *her*.

We didn't have the same types of animals or vegetables they had in their realm, but they were easily substituted for low-level demon meat and whatever roots and vegetables we could find here.

This wasn't the first time I had fed a human, but it was the first time I had been so openly insulted.

There were five dishes in front of her, all of them smelling good to my senses. They might have looked like piles of slop, but surely she would at least try them, right?

"It is," I said, feeling my chest puff. It was good food. I knew that much. And when she finally got over herself and tried it, she would too.

She gave me a look before casting her gaze to the closest bowl. It was stewed demon meat in a bed of grains and a mix of the roots that we dug up here for flavor. All of it human-safe.

"It's almost like you're trying to woo me or something," she muttered, waving her hand around and gesturing to the room. "First you invite me to eat with you in the dining room, and *now* you even prepare a feast?"

I shifted in my chair, casting my gaze to my own bowl. It was very different from hers. Broiled demon meat, though unlike hers, mine hadn't come from the herbivores that roamed the realms where we purchased our meat. Mine came from carnivores. The tougher meat that would give me more sustenance to replace what I was missing by excluding humans from my diet.

Maybe she's disgusted by my food?

Besides the point. Not sure about wooing, but I was trying to... thank her?

I wondered if she knew how much her words on the cliff meant to me. How the acceptance of my realm and *me* meant to me—to someone who had been relatively alone for centuries with no one to converse with.

No one to share this world with.

"Humans eat meals together," I said. "And I was thinking we could start as well."

When I peeked up at her, there was a delightful coloring to her cheeks and ears that caused my stomach to flip.

My mind kept trying to remind me that Mia was only here to reach *her*, something she had not done yet, and that all of this was going overboard.

But I couldn't stop myself.

Especially not when she looks like that.

She tucked a lock of hair behind her ear and lifted her fork.

With hesitant movements, she picked up the tiniest bit of stewed meat and sniffed it.

"I can promise you it's safe," I vowed, my voice laced with just the slightest bit of annoyance.

She narrowed her eyes at me. When I motioned for her to take a bite, she took a deep breath, then shoveled the food into her mouth.

She froze for almost thirty seconds. Panic rose in me.

Does she hate it?

I followed the recipe I remembered. And the demons I chose were similar to the fluffy white herbivores they had in the Human Realm.

Then she began chewing. Wide eyes and a shocked expression met me.

"Wait, that's... that's not bad."

Pride swelled so powerfully in my chest I was worried it might burst. I couldn't keep the smile off my face.

"I know," I said and used my fingers to grab bits of meat from my bowl. She watched me eat with an intense gaze. The meat was tasty, but nothing compared to the memory of Mia's taste on my tongue. "What?"

A small smile spread across her face.

"This is nice," she said with a shrug. "I like eating with you instead of being locked in my room on my own."

"You're not *locked*—"

"Bad choice of words." She raised her hands in a surrendering gesture. "I just mean it's nice to have company. And I'm sure after so long you feel the same. Unless you usually eat with that other demon."

I shook my head.

"We don't eat together," I said. "Like the others, we keep our distance. She does her job, and that's it."

She frowned and looked around the room. "Maybe you should invite her next time."

"And have her eat you instead?" I asked, cocking my head. I didn't mean for it to come out harsh, but the dip in her smile told me it did. "I just want to keep you safe," I supplied hastily.

She nodded and returned her attention to her food.

"I thought that maybe if you find your time here lonely, she might as well," she said. "It wouldn't hurt to try."

I nodded. If it were anyone else, I would have brushed them off. Maybe even fought them for even suggesting *I* was ever lonely in the first place.

But since the day she arrived, I found myself opening up to her in a way I hadn't with anyone before.

Including the humans.

It was like I couldn't stop myself. Like the words just flew out of me, and I only realized what I had said when she looked at me with that small smile of hers.

It means trouble.

And yet I wasn't sure if I wanted to fight it.

CHAPTER 12
MIA

Night had fallen when I heard it.

The rustling of feet down the hallway.

It had been almost a week since I had come to the Demon Realm, and there was no sign of the "ghost" Aris wanted me to reach out to, even though she assured me *she* was probably here.

Multiple times I had wanted to come clean. To tell her that it was all a farce. But I couldn't bring myself to. Not when she was sharing so much with me.

I originally thought the sounds were the various demons that might have been staying in the house, but when the pounding started, I found myself frozen in my bed. Fear overtook me. It clogged my throat and tied me to the bed.

"Aris?" I called into the darkness.

The only answer I got was a pause in the pounding. Then it started again, though this time it was harder, more frenzied. Like they were trying to break down the wall.

"Aris!"

It was mere seconds later that I heard her footsteps down the short hallway between our rooms. Then, my door was flung open.

Light flooded the room—just enough for me to catch sight of Aris's disheveled hair and robe. She wore the same one she always did, but this time it was open, giving me a view of perfect breasts.

I averted my gaze to her eyes. They were glowing a dull red.

"Are you hurt?"

I shook my head. Embarrassment flooded me. Suddenly, I felt like I shouldn't have called her. Especially when she rushed in like *that*.

"Someone was pounding on the walls," I said, pushing myself up to a sitting position.

She looked around the room with a frown. She was still breathing heavily, but the redness in her eyes was fading.

"I didn't hear anything," she murmured. "Are you sure it's not a ghost? Maybe you finally called her?"

I gritted my teeth. *I can't fucking see them*, I almost said.

Instead, I shook my head.

"Ghosts can't touch things like that."

It was a lie, but she didn't see through it. She just nodded and turned to look out onto the hallway.

"Well, whatever it is, I can't see, hear, or smell it," she said.

Fear shot through me.

Was this something that could get past even her?

And if something got past her, what would that mean for me?

"I'm sure I heard it," I said, sitting up on my knees and ready to go to her. She motioned for me to stay put.

"I believe you."

Her words warmed my chest and shattered my heart at the same time.

You shouldn't. Out of all people, it would be easier if you didn't trust me.

She stepped out into the hallway, and my stomach lurched.

"Can you stay?" I asked, my voice shaky. "Please?"

She looked over her shoulder at me. From the expression on her face, I wasn't sure if she would, but she surprised me by nodding and turning back.

"I can smell your fear." She closed the door and came to stand at the foot of my bed. I gripped my night slip nervously.

"Sorry," I murmured. "I'll try to turn it down."

"No." There was a slight growl in that word. "It's not that it's feeding my frenzy. It's uncomfortable in a different way. I don't like you to feel this way."

Oh god, please don't say things like that.

Things that made me like a demon far more than I should. I already felt bad enough for everything she had gone through, and now this?

I shouldn't feel like this about her. I shouldn't feel bad for a creature who could tear my kind apart with her teeth. I shouldn't feel bad for the demon who almost did the same to me.

But as I sat there, crisscrossed on my bed while she stood, her eyebrows pulled together tightly and a frown on her face, I couldn't help the emotions that swirled inside me.

"Talk about something," I all but begged. Trying to distract myself from her. Trying to stop my eyes from moving to her chest again.

She seemed to have no qualms about her nudity, but it was making my stomach warm.

Another emotion I couldn't chance.

"What do you want me to talk about?" she asked. When she cocked her head to the side, her long hair fell off her shoulder.

She usually kept it braided back and out of her face. This was the first time I was seeing it down.

"Her," I forced out, even though I wanted nothing to do with the other human that took up space in her mind. "Tell me about the human you want to contact. Maybe if it is her, I can use the connection."

Lie. Lie. Lie.

But it was what I needed. A reminder of why I was here. It made me feel like a completely shitty person, but that was the point. So that I wouldn't let my mind go wild with thoughts of Aris.

"I'd rather talk about your payment instead," she said, her frown deepening.

"You'd treated me well enough," I replied. "And if you want me to get this done, I need you to tell me more about her."

She shook her head.

"I have treated you as I would any other human, but that doesn't change the fact that what you are helping me with is something worthy of payment."

"I told you I don't need it." I forced out a sigh. "You've been very good to me. Taken me out, given me delicious food, even clothes! I literally could not ask for a better demon."

"You could," she said, her voice filling with venom. "You could ask for a demon who wouldn't hold you hostage. For a demon who would save you. Save your human friends. Just because I am treating you as a guest and not a pet doesn't mean you should get complacent."

Yeah, it would be fucking nice if you just let me go. But I'm also lying about seeing your ghost girlfriend, so I'm not one to talk here.

I knew there was something hidden in those words. Something about how much she loathed herself, but I didn't let myself dwell on it. I couldn't. Because if I did, I might never get out of here. And in order to convince her I was the real deal, I needed to know about this goddamn human.

If we were in the human world, I would have gone on social media. Stalked her a bit. Googled her. Tried to piece her life together.

But in this realm, I had to rely on Aris. And she wasn't giving me nearly enough for me to sell it.

"Fine. I'll let you know when I think of some kind of payment." I offered her a smile. "But *truly*, it would help me if you told me more about her."

She let out a huff and crossed her arms over her chest, slightly covering her self.

"You can't just see her walking around or something?" Aris asked.

I couldn't stop myself from laughing.

"*No*, I can't just see her walking around. I have to pull on her spirit. And how can I do that if I don't know who she is? How do I know which of the many spirits I feel brushing upon me is hers?"

"You can feel them all?"

Shit.

"Yeah," I said, though my confidence dipped when her eyes narrowed. "I mean, you were the one who mentioned soul pieces, right? So you know that a human soul can be anywhere they've been. Including attached to the person—demon—who ate them."

Her face relaxed just enough for my heart to slow down in my chest.

"I haven't eaten that many," she muttered.

I raised an eyebrow at her. "How many in total?"

"Won't it scare you?" she shot back.

I sighed. "I told you on the cliffs that I can't hold it against you. Just tell me."

Her jaw tightened, and I could hear her teeth grinding in the quiet room.

"Three hundred," she finally replied. "Back when I was young, I would let myself indulge maybe once or twice a year, but as I got older, I skipped years altogether. The more powerful the human, the more power they had, the longer they would sustain me."

I nodded, biting my bottom lip.

Don't ask, please don't ask, just shut—

"How long did she last?"

"Twenty years," she answered. "But I didn't get any powers from her."

"You can take our powers?"

She gave me a stiff nod. "They help with the hunger. Though sometimes, if you're lucky, the power will transfer to you. I was not. Another reason I wouldn't chance eating you."

Oh geez, how thoughtful.

"So, what do you eat now?"

My mind went back to our time in the dining room together. It looked like a bunch of burnt meat, but I didn't allow myself to wonder what kind of meat it could be.

She looked away.

"What?" I demanded. "What could be worse than eating humans?"

"Eating other demons," she said. Her eyes shot to me as if she were almost afraid of what my reaction would be.

"Demons like your maids or demons like hellhounds?" I asked.

She didn't want to smile, but I saw her lips twitching. "We don't have hellhounds here. But yes, something similar. They don't always taste that good."

"But it's still a way for you to stop yourself from eating me and other humans. Nothing to be ashamed about." I leaned back on my pillow, placing my hands behind me and tilting my head. "I'm guessing not all demons think like you."

She gave me a shrug.

"I guess I'm lucky then," I said on a smile.

Something like happiness showed on her face, and it shouldn't have made me feel the way it did. I opened my mouth to change the subject, but then I felt a strong force swirling around the room. I snapped my head to the right and toward the aura, expecting to see one of those gruesome monsters from the auction house again.

But instead, there was nothing.

"Did you see something?" she asked.

Damn it. Maybe I should just come clean. Whatever was in this house wasn't a fucking ghost. And the more I tried to pretend it was, the more danger I could be in.

"Listen, I have to tell you something. I—"

My throat clogged and the blood in my veins froze when I caught sight of a flash of white behind her.

CHAPTER 13

MIA

This one was so much worse than the one in the auction house.

Yes, she was skeleton-like, but the skin that she had left on her was grayish. The hair that had once covered her head stuck out around her on all sides and flowed as if she were underwater. There was a cloth wrapped around her arms, chest, and waist that seemed stained with blood. That, too, was floating around her.

My attention was fully focused on her, and when Aris moved to look back at whatever I was seeing, I got a full look at the girl's mutilated body and ripped-up face. I could just make out her eyes and gaping mouth, but everything else was unrecognizable.

I tried to push myself back as far as I could and yelped when my back slammed against the headboard.

"What is it?" Aris asked. "Do you see what it is? What do you see? Is she here? Cara?"

She looked around the room, not noticing the being that was right behind her.

Aris can't see her.

"Cara, is that you?" she tried again, but the being paid her no mind. Instead, she just stared straight at me.

"Hel—," she started, and her voice came out gargled. "Help me."

"Shit," I muttered under my breath. "What does Cara look like?" I asked Aris, not daring to take my eyes away from whatever the apparition was.

"Yellow hair, green eyes," Aris forced out, still frantically searching for the ghost that was staring directly at me.

Disappointment hit me straight in the gut. Even with her changed body, I could tell this was not Cara.

"It's not her," I forced out a scream that got caught in my throat when the being pushed forward and put her bony hands on the bed.

"What do you mean it's not her?" Aris asked, her voice dropping.

"Don't come closer," I warned. Aris's gaze snapped toward me.

"What happening? Where is she?" she asked in a growl her eyes searching across the room.

The moan that came out of the being's mouth caused all my hair to stand on edge.

"Help me," she pleaded again.

When her hand shot forward to wrap around my ankle, I opened my mouth to scream, but no words came out.

Memories that weren't mine forced themselves into my head. Memories of a human life so unlike my own. I saw her with her family at home. The eldest daughter simply on the way home from work when the demons had taken her.

I watched as she spent months on end at the auction house, being assessed by potential buyers as if she were some—thing. They looked at her, watched her as she slept, made comments on her body shape.

It had been hell for her. Until the day of the auction.

I can't watch this.

I saw Aris in her mind. She looked so much like she had the night she bought me. Then a flash of Aris's bloodstained face and red eyes hit me. The frenzied version of her was attacking me. *No—* she was attacking the girl.

Image after image of Aris losing control was forced into my mind. It was disorientating, especially when I knew how much it had to have hurt Aris as well.

"Aris, please," I choked out, trying to reach for the demon. "Aris, help. Please, god. Make it stop."

Even without knowing what I was seeing or why I was afraid, she didn't hesitate to wrap her arms around me, one behind my back, one under my legs, and lift me up and away from the bed. When she yanked me away, the woman's memories started to fade. The being was too slow to grip onto me as we pulled away, but she sure as hell tried.

Her head slowly turned toward us, and whiplash from the memories caused bile to rise in my throat. I had to grab on to Aris to steady myself.

"What does she look like?" Aris asked, pulling me further away from the memories.

That's right. This Aris is different. This isn't the one you saw.

"Black hair." I tried to squint and make out the eyes. "I think the eyes are brown. I can't tell. Her face is—" I couldn't even describe it. "Oh my gosh. It's awful."

Aris cursed under her breath and all but ran out of there with me in her arms. As soon as we left the room, I felt like I could breathe again. Her aura wasn't sticking to me and the memories had almost disappeared, but the image of Aris's frenzied face lingered.

"That's not a ghost," I said, peering back behind us.

I could still hear her moans, but she didn't follow us.

"That's not Cara," Aris said. "I won't know who exactly it is without some sort of picture, but I'm assuming it's one of the other ones I ate."

One of the other ones.

The girl had been mutilated, so much so I could barely make out her facial features. Was that how the person who was now holding me had treated humans?

My first instinct was to ask her to put me down, but I pushed my lips together in a thin line.

She never lied to you. You knew about this.

As if she knew what was on my mind, her warm touch turned scalding.

"You're staying with me tonight."

"Is that something you had made or…?" I trailed off as I took in the sight of the contraption Aris tied to her face.

She stood at the foot of the bed, her chest puffed and hands on her hips. Pride was radiating off her even if I couldn't make out the bottom half of her face, which was now covered by a thick leather-like fabric. Straps held it in place and wrapped around the back of her head, disappearing into her long hair that was now flowing against her almost bare back.

She had changed into a loose tank top-like shirt that could hardly be called a tank top with the amount of skin it showed. My eyes kept trailing to her barely concealed nipples, but the elephant in the room kept pulling my attention away from her breasts.

"It's necessary if you are to be staying in here with me," she said, then turned her back to me and lifted the top half of her hair up. In the middle of her head, attached to the mask, was a glowing blue crystal. "Touch it. Then it will only come off if *you* take it off."

"That's a lot of trust," I muttered before shakily kneeling on her bed. She stayed still as I crawled toward her.

It had been hours since the encounter with that… *thing*, and most of the memories had faded, except for the image of Aris with blood splattered on her face.

It scared me, of course it did. But it also made me so incredibly sad for her.

"I meant it when I said I didn't want to hurt you," she whispered.

The hand that had unconsciously reached out for the crystal paused.

"You can still kill me without the muzzle," I said.

A beat of silence passed between us.

"Yes," she admitted in a low voice. "But the frenzy wants to feed, not just kill. If anything, I would try to persuade you to take it off."

I swallowed thickly and let my fingers brush across the crystal.

A low burst of heat exploded from the rock and shot down my arm. The straps tightened around her face. She turned back around and let her hair down. The muzzle was stretched against her skin and only had a few holes to allow her to breathe.

I reached out and let my fingers trace the seams. Feeling every bump on the thick fabric. She groaned when I forced my fingers between the fabric and her skin, but made no move to stop me.

I shouldn't be doing this. Being so casual with her. Imagining what could happen next. But I couldn't stop myself.

Not even when I knew how much of a monster she had once been.

"That defeats the purpose," she growled.

With a smile, I tugged harshly at it, causing her to jerk forward.

"Just making sure I won't wake up with your teeth buried in my shoulder."

A light flashed across her eyes before her eyebrows pulled together.

"Maybe it would be better if I stayed elsewhere tonight," she said. "You might not end up with my teeth in you, but... who knows what I might do when I'm half asleep?"

I fell back to the bed, letting go of her muzzle.

"I need you near me in case that... *thing* comes back," I replied, trying to suppress a shiver.

"My guess is that it's either a wraith or a phantom, neither of which my kind can see, though I've heard of them," Aris offered as an explanation and started to climb onto the bed.

The action forced me backwards involuntarily, my heart pounding in my chest. Aris's face twisted.

When I stayed still, she slowly crawled toward me on her hands and knees, her long hair brushing against the bed. When she finally got close enough, she placed her hands on either side of me and leaned forward.

"I'm sorry," she murmured, though the look in her eyes told me the opposite. "You smell really good."

Her words caused my entire body to heat.

Shit. Her eyes flashed red for a second telling me she could smell just how turned on I was.

"Don't tell me you like the muzzle," she teased, leaning forward to rub the contraption against the crook of my neck.

"Is this the frenzy talking?" I asked. My breathing came heavier then, and with each breath, my erect nipples brushed across her chest. She was so close I could feel the heat radiating off her skin.

"No," she said with a growl. "Something else."

Heat blossomed in my lower belly.

"I thought—"

"I didn't want to hurt you," she cut me off before moving her muzzled mouth up toward my ear and whispering, "But now that I can't, *and* your scent tells me how much you like the sight, I think I want something *else* from you tonight."

"And if I say I don't?"

She let out a husky chuckle and pulled away. Listening to her desire-filled voice and the way her eyes flashed while her mouth was muzzled did something to me. Maybe it was the control aspect of it. Knowing *I* was the only one who could release her. Knowing *I* was the one bringing her to the brink of a madness I didn't quite understand just yet.

She leaned forward again, as if to kiss me, before inhaling deeply. I lifted my chin, but instead of pushing her muzzle to my lips, she trailed down to my chest, pausing to inhale again.

My breath caught.

She's not going to do what I think she is, is she?

When her muzzled mouth brushed against my breast, all thoughts left my mind. Her eyes trailed up to mine as she lowered herself between my legs.

I was still wearing the thin slip I wore to bed with just a thin pair of panties under it. She pushed my legs apart, a low snarl falling from her lips when she caught sight of my clothed pussy.

"Lift your dress for me, human."

With a shaky hand, I did as she said. Her fingers hooked onto the straps of my underwear before pulling it apart. The tearing sound echoed through the room.

I let out a gasp when the cool leather of her muzzle pushed against my wet cunt. She inhaled again.

"If I inhale deeply enough, I can just make out your taste," she groaned. The veins had appeared again, and her eyes were now flashing wildly. More red was seeping into them, warning me of what was to come.

"Your frenzy—"

"Frenzy or not, I plan to fuck you tonight, Mia," she warned. "No matter how much I plead and beg, don't take off the muzzle."

I reached out and pulled her forward. Her loud warning growl sent a shock of heat to my core. Evidence of my arousal coated her muzzle and gleamed in the darkness, so I swiped my tongue across it. My own taste burst across my tongue.

I could feel the push of her tongue on the other side of the muzzle, desperately trying to savor me.

Tell her, the sane part of my mind ordered me. *Tell her you're lying.*

Guilt and shame filled my chest. The sound of her calling out the ghost of her last companion swirled around my head.

I can still back out. And knowing the demon in front of me, she probably would have understood.

But the way my pussy was throbbing was too delicious to ignore. I never thought myself to be a good person, so why would I change that now?

"Delicious," I muttered, looking up at her through my lashes. "But I know for a fact you will taste even better."

CHAPTER 14

ARIS

y hands fisted the blankets, a tearing sound seeping through the air as my claws extended and ripped through the cloth.

Growls rumbled through my chest, and low whines fell from my lips.

Mia's hands gripped my thighs, forcing them to stay put on her shoulders while she feasted on my cunt. She wasted no time trying to bring me to an orgasm, and it took every ounce of self-control I had in me to stay still.

But with each lap of her tongue, I felt the thread holding me back get thinner and thinner.

Don't hurt her.

"Are you holding back on me?" she asked, peering up at me. I screwed my eyes open to catch sight of her mischievous gaze and wet lips.

"I don't want to hurt you," I panted.

She trailed fiery kisses up my thigh before coming back to drag her tongue between my folds. When her lips circled my clit and sucked it into her mouth, I almost lost it as I bucked against her. It had been so long since anyone had touched me like this that it would be mere moments until I was coming in her mouth.

I could feel her eyes on my face, watching as I struggled to regain composure. That seemed to empower her, and she doubled her efforts, flattening her tongue and licking me bottom to clit.

I felt it from head to toe as a powerful wave of pleasure shot through me.

"Just like that," I moaned. I pried my hand from the shredded blankets to tangle them through her hair, fisting it, but being careful to retract my claws so I wouldn't risk nicking her.

As she sucked on my clit harder, my entire body curled into her.

"Oh, fuck, yes, just like that."

Her grip on my thighs tightened, and she scraped her teeth against my swollen bundle of nerves, whispering, "*Ah*, good girl. So fucking good—"

I couldn't take it anymore. I came with a cry, using my hand to bring her closer so I could ride her face through the waves of a powerful orgasm. My pussy clenched around nothing, and my teeth ached unbearably. The need to bite down into her soft flesh was almost too much.

When she pulled away, I grabbed her and turned us around, so I was on top. I pushed my muzzled mouth into the flesh of her neck and grumbled in frustration when I found myself unable to tear through the muzzle.

Her arms wrapped around me, and her legs instantly fell open. Without waiting a single moment, I pushed my fingers through her folds, moaning as they met her wetness.

Her scent had permeated the room and was overpowering all. The frenzy was tickling the edges of my mind, and before I knew it, I was begging.

"Let me taste you, Mia," I whispered against the muzzle as I nuzzled her neck. She gasped when I pushed two fingers into her wet cunt, and I moaned at the heat around my fingers.

She was so wet and ready for me, it had me salivating.

"Maybe if you make me come, I'll consider it," she said with a light laugh.

I let out a frustrated growl and began pumping my fingers into her hard. Her soft body arched into me, and her laughs quickly turned to moans.

I paid extra attention to her cues. The way her pussy clenched when my thumb brushed across her clit. The way her hands tugged at my hair when I curled them inside her.

With each moan that fell from her lips and each spasm of her cunt around my fingers, I found myself falling deeper and deeper into her. For the first time, the frenzy was chased away and replaced with a visceral need to pleasure her until she couldn't stand it anymore.

I longed to hear my name fall from her lips.

"Don't stop," she panted against me.

I won't.

I can't.

Not until I had fed this new hunger inside me. Thoughts of Cara left my mind and were replaced by *her*. Mia. It wasn't surprising; it had been like this for days now. I should have realized how far I had fallen. Realized just how much I had come to care for this human in the short time that she had been here.

"You feel so good," I moaned and flexed my fingers inside her. Her hips jerked to meet my thrusts and her grip on me slackened. I pulled my head from the crook of her neck to watch her come.

Her mouth was propped open, her eyes squeezed shut. Her eyebrows were pulled together. Sweat lined her forehead. Her chest heaved with each breath.

Perfect.

She cried out as her pussy tightened around my digits, and I made sure to take note of every single thing her body did as she came.

I paused for a moment, transfixed by the way pleasure overtook her. Wishing I could stick my tongue inside her.

Then, I continued fucking her.

I need to watch her come again.

"Wait—"

She tried to protest, but I fit another finger inside her and curled them, turning whatever she was about to say into a whine.

"Again, Mia," I commanded. "This time, call my name when you come. Scream it. Let everyone in this realm know how much you like it when I'm fucking you?"

CHAPTER 15

MIA

Clawed hands gripped my hips and pushed me against the cold counter.

There was a sharp burst of pain that shot through my body, but it was nothing in comparison to the heat that Aris started inside me.

Her hands alone could send shivers up my spine, but the brush of her lips on the back of my neck caused my entire body to melt into her.

Over the last few weeks, she had been careful not to let her unmuzzled mouth anywhere near my skin, but it looked like tonight she was making an exception to that rule.

And after everything that had been happening with the sightings, I welcomed the distraction.

"My bed was cold when I woke up," she murmured against my skin.

The heat that rose to my face was embarrassing. I should have been trying to find a way to get out of this situation. I thought about faking finding her ex-companion, but I couldn't do that to her.

And the longer I stayed entangled with her, the harder it became.

"You sleep too much," I said and turned around to face her.

Ever since our night together, she had given up trying to prim herself in the morning for me and instead just let herself *literally* roll out of bed.

Her long hair was tangled around her head. Her eyes still heavy with sleep. And the robe she had haphazardly thrown on was falling off her shoulders and gave me a perfect view of the grayish skin of her chest.

I gave into the urge to push my cheek against it, reveling in the warmth.

"Can I tell you something?" she murmured, her lips coming to brush the top of my head.

I leaned back to look at her and caught a small smile that took my breath away.

"Anything," I breathed.

She ran a clawed hand through my hair.

"I can't remember the last time I slept so well."

Her confession caused my throat to close up and tears to prick my eyes.

Damn it.

"Even through the many rude awakenings?" I asked, trying to keep my voice light.

She let out a huff of a laugh.

"Well, the night before *was* a bit much," she said. "I expected maybe one or two wraiths here or there, not *three* in one night."

I cringed, remembering the way their moans had pulled me from my sleep. It hadn't taken Aris long to figure out what they were. Especially with the help of some of the people at the auction house. All it took were a few summons for us to realize that I was seeing wraiths, not ghosts.

I felt a bit of relief when I heard that. Meaning that, even though I was lying about *something*, there was still a surprise power inside me. The only issue was that Aris was sure her old companion would never have become a wraith.

Apparently, you needed to harbor some very powerful, angry emotions to become a wraith, and per Aris's word, she had been far too depressed to become anything but a ghost.

"Well, at least your friend is coming to get rid of them, right?" I asked, hope burning my chest.

If we could get someone to get rid of these wraiths, I would have an excuse for Aris. I planned to tell her that her companion had to have been taken out with the others.

But even that excuse brought a sour taste to my mouth.

"Not a friend. But yes, she'll be here any min—"

Black smoke burst into the kitchen, shrouding the entire place in a glittery darkness.

Aris turned around to shield me. Her arms wrapped around me and pulled me behind her. I peeked over her shoulder to catch sight of the same demon who had been at the auction house.

A creature that melted into the shadows seemed out of pace in the well-lit kitchen.

The first time I had seen her, I had been far too scared to even take a good look at her. She looked as though she was literally born from the shadows. Her black hair disappeared into the ones that surrounded her. Her eyes were all black, save for small white pupils that were now narrowed in on me.

Her horns were a deep purple with jewels embedded in them. She wore a robe similar to Aris's, but I couldn't help but let my gaze wander to her bare, clawed feet.

"Iris asked me to greet you, human," Yien said, her tone almost hollow.

The news of Iris still being alive *and* remembering that I even existed caused something to unclench in my chest. I was too focused on my own survival to see where ethe other two went, but I was happy it was with this demon.

"I hope you've been treating her well," I said with a raised brow. I might have gotten lucky with my demon, but not everyone would. Even though, from what Aris had told me, she had gone through a lot of trouble to win Iris.

Yien gave me a stiff nod.

"Food, water, a bed, and daily walks in the light," she replied. "Everything a human needs."

I bristled at her words.

"She's not a pet," I hissed.

Yien tilted her head. "She is like one, no?"

I tried to go around Aris, ready to hit Yien with a word vomit explanation of why it was demeaning, but my demon held me back.

"Later," she whispered to me before looking at Yien. "I need your help banishing wraiths. Apparently, this manor is *filled* with them."

Yien tilted her head to the side.

"Of course," she said, unsurprised. "But why banish them? If they don't bother you—"

"I see them," I said quickly. "And they can touch me."

Yien's brows pulled together.

"And you can actually feel them?" she asked.

"Yes," I said with a small frown. I said they touched me. Wasn't that clear enough?

"Does it hurt?" she prodded further. "Burning pain or anything like that?"

I shook my head. I wasn't ready to tell Aris about what I saw in case she pulled away from me. I could see how much it affected her when she thought I was scared of her. If she knew that I saw what she had done to them in their last moments, how would she react?

Aris's hand ghosted my back.

"It's been getting bad recently," she said. "Like she's calling to them somehow."

Yien's eyes were still locked on me, causing a light sheen of sweat to coat my skin. Her scrutiny was hard to bear.

"I see," she mused, her gaze calculating. "That *is* worrisome."

She stayed silent, as if waiting for me to jump in. The constant pressure from her gaze combined with the swirling smoke around us caused my heart rate to spike, and I knew both of them could hear just how much she was affecting me.

"You're scaring her," Aris snapped.

Yien's head tilted to the side, her almost all black eyes shooting toward her.

"She's doing that herself," Yien said, though there was no anger in her tone. She seemed... amused. "Get annoyed with her, not me."

My gaze moved to Aris just as hers met mine.

"Is something wrong?" she asked. "The smell of your fear is very—"

"Overwhelming," Yien finished for her. "Though I am surprised how well Aris is handling it."

Aris sent her a look but chose not to respond.

I swallowed thickly and sent Aris a forced smile. "Nothing. The faster we get rid of the wraiths, the better."

———

With an open mouth I watched as Yien banished wraith after wraith.

All of them had been hovering around my previous room. Maybe Aris had been right, and all this time I had acted like a beacon for them. Maybe if I had just ignored the pounding on the walls that night, they might not have noticed me. But since then, their presence has only grown stronger.

Plus, if I had, the rest of the night wouldn't have happened either. And I didn't regret that.

Even though the rooms were close, the wraiths never entered Aris's room. At night, their moans and pounding would wake me up, but they wouldn't get close enough to touch me with Aris by my side.

Maybe the memories of what Aris did to them were still too fresh for them to dare get near her.

There were about eleven in the hallway alone and a few more in the bedroom. Yien wasted no time using her shadows to wrap them in cocoons of darkness, squeezing until they disappeared entirely.

Even as Yien was destroying them, the hallway was thick with the dark aura that surrounded them. It was enough to make my stomach twist.

"Does it hurt?" I asked.

"No," Yien responded, not even bothering to turn to look back at me. "The only pain they feel is emotional. Once they're banished to the Shadow Realm, their soul will wander there until it too perishes."

I swallowed thickly. This would be hell for Iris as someone who saw emotional auras. I wondered if she could feel them as well.

I moved to follow Yien as she entered the room, but Aris's firm hand on my elbow held me back.

"Let her deal with it," she said, her voice low enough so the demon would hear her. "I know seeing them distresses you."

I grimaced.

"Is it that obvious?" I asked with a nervous laugh.

"Very," she answered. "Fear is particularly easy to smell. It excites the frenzy."

I bit my bottom lip hard enough to clear my mind of the fear she so accurately pegged, but that wasn't the only thing bothering me.

"It's hard not to feel bad for them," I admitted. "It's not just fear but also—"

"You feel for them," she finished for me. "Your fellow species. And you know I am the one to blame. You see how I tore apart their flesh. How I consumed them."

Her words caused my entire body to stiffen. Even without their memories, I would still have been able to see it. The claw marks left on their skin. The way some of their heads were holding on by thin scraps of flesh.

It was horrific.

How could I not feel for them?

"Do you resent me?" she asked. "For what I did to them? For what I could do to you?"

No, was what I wanted to say, but no words came out. There was something deeper in her question. Something that I needed to answer for myself as well.

If I don't resent her, what do I feel for her?

We didn't just fuck—we slept together, had our meals together, spent time together. She told me things she had never told anyone before... So where did that leave us?

"Alright," Yien said, breaking the awkward silence. "Now let's take a look at the rest of the house."

Aris didn't seem pleased, but she let me go. And I was thankful for it.

CHAPTER 16

MIA

Do you resent me?

The words circled my mind over and over again with no reprieve. We just watched as Yien went through the house, destroying six more wraiths before she went back to her world.

We had days together where we just... *lived.* Days of sleeping next to Aris in the most restful sleep I had gotten since coming here. Days of traveling her realm. Days of trying new foods. Days of listening to her stories and learning that, although she was a demon, we might not be that different in the end.

We hadn't talked about Cara. Nor had we mentioned anything about the humans she had murdered. We ignored all the obvious things that threatened the peace we had here.

But still, I couldn't get her words out of my mind.

Even as her arms wrapped around me and her lips trailed my shoulder, I couldn't stop thinking. I didn't resent her, but I couldn't put my emotions into words either.

The real question was... *Would she resent* me?

After she found out that I had lied to her, then what? Would she feel betrayed? Would she be angry?

She might end up being both, but I somehow knew that she would do anything in her power to keep me safe anyway.

"What if we never make contact?" I asked, my voice barely above a whisper.

We were in her bedroom again. We were supposed to be sleeping, but we never really cared to. Not when my body seemed to hum whenever she even so much as brushed her hand against my skin.

She stalled before her hand grabbed my thigh and hooked it over her leg, opening me so my pussy was bared to her. The image of her between my legs only caused me to grow wetter.

Nothing could stop my reaction to her. Not wraiths. Not ghosts of her old companions. Nothing.

We didn't bother with clothes in bed anymore. And now that Aris had gotten used to my scent, she hadn't needed the muzzle.

I gasped when her hand touched my cunt. My body was always ready for her to play with. It didn't matter the time of day nor how many times we had already fucked, as soon as her hands brushed my hips or her lips trailed kisses on my neck, I was already melting for her.

It made this whole thing that much harder.

"Then I'll have an excuse to keep you here," she whispered. Her fingers brushed across my clit teasingly.

My heart skipped a beat. *An excuse.*

"You would keep me?" I asked. She hummed against my skin. My nipples raised to points at the sound, and a shaky breath forced itself from my lips.

"Is it wrong for me to want to?" she asked. "I haven't felt like this in decades. I can't imagine this realm without you." She paused, her hands trailing down my cunt before teasing my wet entrance. "Unless you want to leave me?"

She pushed her fingers in just enough to tease me, but not enough to give me any relief. My clit was swollen and aching, just begging for her touch. I tried to buck against her, but she wouldn't move.

"Tell me, *Mia*."

God, the way my name sounded from her lips was enough to cause my head to spin.

Of course I want to leave... right?

I had a cat, a shop, a *life* to get back to. Aris had been so open about giving me the chance to go back there from the start that there was no reason to believe she was lying about it.

"Aris, I—"

My voice cut out when she forced two fingers inside me. She wasn't gentle this time as she fucked me. She knew how to make me come after weeks of being together, and she employed all the tricks she had learned. Her tongue trailed my skin. Her fingers circled inside me. Her thumb abused my engorged clit.

"Your pause tells me everything I need to know," her voice had turned hard. "Don't worry, I'll fuck you good until then. So even when you leave here, you'll still find yourself aching for me."

I cried out as my orgasm hit me faster than it ever had before. I shook against her as my pussy clamped down on her fingers, but even as I came, she made no move to stop. If anything, she picked up the pace.

"Aris, too much—"

She covered my mouth with hers. Something she hadn't done since the first night.

Her tongue explored my mouth. Her kiss was harsh, like all she wanted to do was dominate me. She was trying to keep true to her words. She never *ever* wanted me to forget what happened here.

When she pulled away, I was breathless. Spit connected our mouths, the sight of it causing me to clench around her fingers.

"I need to taste," she said in a voice akin to a whine.

"*Please.*"

My brain told me I shouldn't let her. That I should push her away. But instead, I was quiet as she turned me onto my stomach and pulled my hips into the air.

Her breath fanned across my cunt and caused my hands to fist the sheets underneath us.

"You smell divine," she groaned.

The first brush of her tongue was light. A test for herself as she paused behind me. I waited for her to tell me she couldn't do this, but then her tongue trailed from my clit to my ass.

I cried out, pushing my hips back to get more of that delightful tongue.

"Fuck," I moaned as it plunged inside me.

She was thorough as she devoured me. No place was left untouched. She made sure to clean up every bit of wetness I was leaking.

I could tell her actions were more about herself. So that she could finally get a taste of what had been teasing her the entire time we had been together. But even so, she took good care of me.

She always did.

When I used my hands to pluck my nipples, she groaned against my cunt before reaching under me and doing it herself.

"You taste even better than I imagined," she moaned. She gave me a long lick before forcing two fingers inside. My walls fluttered around her fingers, warning me of what was to come.

"So sweet. So intoxicating." She thrust her fingers into me with each word. The slam of her fist against me caused my moans to get stuck in my throat.

I couldn't speak. Couldn't move. All I could feel was her.

The way her fingers pinched my nipple. The way her breath felt against my pussy. The way her fingers pounded into me like they wanted to bruise me. The brush of the sheets against my oversensitive skin, along with the scent of her, was becoming too much.

When she pulled her fingers out of me, I whined, but it was cut short as her tongue lapped up the extra wetness that had gathered.

I was trembling by the time she sucked my clit into her mouth.

I couldn't hold back my orgasm. It hit me without any warning and caused even more wetness to leak from me.

"Oh my god, *Aris*, please don't stop."

She growled but kept up her movements until my orgasm had subsided.

When she pulled back, her fingers replaced her mouth and rubbed slow circles over my clit. It was torture in the best way possible. My entire body was humming, and each movement against the bundle of nerves felt like a bolt of lightning going through me.

"I'm saddened you would want to leave me after we finish up here," she said from behind me.

From my position, I was able to look back at her but couldn't catch the full expression on her face.

"But your companion—"

"She's not here anymore! You are!"

I let out a whine as her fingers stretched me. Four this time while her other hand continued to rub my bundle of nerves.

"Can't you see how much better my life has been since you're here? I even stopped asking you to look for her."

She had. Ever since the day Yien got rid of the wraiths, we hadn't spoken about her previous companions at all, let alone Cara.

And why was that? If she wanted me to find her, why would she give it all up?

"Because I couldn't find her," I spat back.

A low chuckle rumbled in her chest. It only heightened my arousal. She was playing my body like an instrument. Forcing me to fall apart, all while she was there *laughing*.

"Because I didn't *want* you to."

The heat she had been building in my belly grew tenfold at her confession. It was dark and held such power that everything that had been holding me back before vanished.

Because she wants me. That's why she didn't ask me to continue. Because if I find her, I'll leave.

But nothing could dampen the guilt. I should have been happy, but instead all I felt was guilt.

"Aris," I panted. "I have to tell you something."

"Tell me that you're staying?" she asked with a laugh. "All it took was two more orgasms? You should have held out for longer."

"Aris, I—" I took a deep breath and used the fact that she couldn't see my face right now to blurt it all out.

. "I can't see ghosts. That's why I couldn't find her. Because I can't see her."

CHAPTER 17

ARIS

Rage flashed across my mind, and I had to catch myself from sinking my claws into her soft skin.

I took a deep breath.

Then another.

And another.

Was she still talking? If so, I wasn't listening. All I could hear was the ringing in my head and the voice telling me to end it all.

To end *her*.

She lied to me. This entire time.

Why would Mia lie like this?

"But you see wraiths." The words left my mouth before my mind caught up to what I was doing.

She tried to turn around, but I moved fast and gripped her hip with one hand, using the other to clamp down on the back of her neck. I couldn't look at her. Not yet.

Not until my teeth stopped aching and the fog lifted from my mind.

"I was surprised when I saw them," she said, her voice slightly muffled. "I've lied about it for money before, but I never thought—"

"That I would actually need your power?" I asked through gritted teeth.

That was the whole reason she ended up here. I needed her to reach Cara, but that wasn't what hurt me the most.

What hurt me the most was that, even after I had spilled everything to her, after I had ripped open the wall that had kept me safe from grief for the last millennium, she still hadn't trusted me enough to be honest with me.

Have I been wrong this entire time? Am I the only one who feels the pull?

Is that why she still wants to leave?

"That I would be fucking kidnapped!"

Her anger was the thing that caused me to snap back to myself. A coldness washed over me.

Yes. That's right. Above all else, she was still here because she had been stolen from her world. She didn't want to be here.

A dull ache blossomed in my chest.

I knew all that deep inside, but somehow I still allowed myself to wonder. What it would be like if she was stuck here. What it would be like if she *wanted* to be here.

I had fooled myself into thinking I would finally have a companion. But not just any companion. One who wouldn't look at me with the disgust the others had. One who not only accepted me but wanted me.

Of course a part of me was still furious that she had lied, but that was nothing against the growing realization that Mia wouldn't be able to stay here.

That she didn't want to stay here.

And just how awful of a demon I would become if I forced her to be here against her will.

Just like the rest.

Even though I hadn't meant to, I had treated her just like the other humans. It was a heartbreaking realization.

"Look, I'm not sure why you wanted to contact her so badly, but maybe we can try—"

"I wanted to apologize."

My voice sounded hollow even to my own ears. The rage had subsided to a simmer while a tile wave of grief for the person right in front of me hit.

I was going to lose her, and there was nothing I could do about it.

"I—" My throat closed in on itself without permission. "I really did care for her. As a companion. As a lover. Until then, the only one I really cared about, and I thought I was in control. Until I snapped one day and didn't come out of it until she was gone. I wanted to tell her I *never* meant to hurt her."

When the words that had been holding my heart hostage for the last millennium were finally spoken into the world, there was nothing but silence. A cold silence that gave me no indication of whether Cara would ever hear them.

But Mia did. And her light gasp gave me all the answer I needed. She may not resent me, but she could still fear me. And I may have just given her a reason to.

No matter how selfish I wanted to be, I couldn't keep her here. She didn't belong here. And now that the cat was out of the bag, there was no excuse I could use to keep her.

I only wished she kept it to herself for even just five minutes more.

My eyes began to burn.

"Aris, let me—"

"No! Don't look at me!"

I jumped off the bed and stormed out of the room, not caring about my state of undress. No one would care anyway.

CHAPTER 18

MIA

I fucked up.

The one time I tried to tell the truth, it blew up right in my face.

That should teach me to try to be a good person.

Aris had been ignoring me since that night. She didn't even try to come back to her room. I don't know where she's been sleeping, but it hadn't been with me.

Finally, after four days of being ignored, I decided I needed to take matters into my own hands.

"Hey, you."

The demon who had been bending over to put something in the rusty oven jumped and let out a shrill scream that caused me to flinch.

Thera turned to me with wide eyes and a slightly agape mouth.

I had seen her around once or twice since I had gotten here but never had a chance to talk to her. Though based on Aris's reaction the first time we met, I was pretty sure he'd planned for us not to meet. And now I could see why.

Black veins appeared on her forehead, and her eyes began to glow.

The frenzy.

Or at least that's what the demons called it. I should have been worried that she was fighting her instincts to eat me, but after living with Aris for the time I had, I couldn't help but feel for them. They didn't *want* to hurt me. That much was clear.

"Where's Aris?" I asked, crossing my arms over my chest.

She took a step back, her eyes darting around the room.

"You shouldn't be this close to me. It's dangerous."

I rolled my eyes. "The quicker you answer the question, the quicker I'll leave."

She opened her mouth to speak but then snapped it shut and shook her head wildly. Her clawed hand gripped onto the counter behind her, and for the first time in days, fear seized my heart.

I took a step back.

Shit.

I had severely underestimated just how much my presence would affect her.

"Where are you going?" she asked, though her voice didn't sound much like hers anymore. There was a growl to it. Her eyes narrowed at my movements. I took another step back, but she was following me like I was her prey.

Damn it.

"I think I hear Aris," I said, trying to keep my voice calm. "I'll just go to her now."

My heart was beating wildly in my chest, and my throat was closing in on itself. Even if I wanted to scream, I doubt I would have enough time to.

The demon gave me a sharp nod and closed her eyes, the internal fight against herself and her frenzy obvious on her face.

"I can smell your fear, human," she muttered, her eyes still closed. She inhaled deeply.

I took two more steps back. By the time the heel of my foot hit the ground for a third time, her eyes popped open.

Run.

I turned and ran back into the hallway I had come from. I launched myself too hard and ended up slammed into the wall but used it as leverage to push me forward.

Her roar shook the walls around me.

"Run, human! And when I catch you, I'll enjoy tearing your flesh—"

The sound of my heart pulsing in my chest combined with the thuds of my feet against the carpeted floors drowned out her words.

I had spent time exploring this place with Aris, so it was easy to follow the path that led to her room, no matter how many twists and turns the house had.

Until I got to the stairs.

I could hear her running after me. The sound of her flat shoes slapping against the carpet told me that she had crossed the space in half the time it had taken me.

"Aris!" I screamed.

My hand clawed at the banister, trying to use anything in my grasp to pull me up the stairs faster. I used the other to push against the steps, almost like I was crawling up the stairs.

"Found you."

The footsteps stopped when she entered the room with the grand staircase. I shot a panicked look back to see the crazed demon looking at me with a sinister smirk.

The image reminded me too much of what Aris had looked like in the images the wraith had sent me. It caused me to freeze because if *that* was what they saw in their last moments...

Is this to be mine?

She was too close now. I couldn't outrun her.

So instead, I stopped and turned to face her. All the energy to run whooshed out of me, and a crazed giggle fell from my lips.

The wraiths. They tried to warn me, I realized in that moment. They had been warning me to run. Warning me that if I stayed here, *this* would be my ending.

The demon was in front of me in a flash. Her teeth bared, her eyes wide, her clawed hands on either side of me, trapping me between her arms.

What I didn't expect were the tears that filled her eyes. Without thinking, I lifted my hand to cup her cheek.

"I know it's hard," I whispered.

Her snarling paused, and for a second, it looked like she might back off.

Until a hand gripped her shoulders and flung her back, and arms wrapped around me and forced me upright.

Aris's growl was so loud her chest vibrated with it. I looked up to see her staring down to where she had thrown the other demon.

"I will kill you," she vowed.

Thera's whimper caused my gaze to shoot to her. She lay crumpled on the hard floor below us, her leg twisted painfully. Aris shifted against me, as if she really was going to go and finish the job.

I put a hand on her chest.

"Please. Don't hurt her," I pleaded.

She didn't even spare me a glance.

"I will do what I must."

Ice cold fear froze the blood in my veins. I pushed her away and gripped the railing behind me.

Her eyes finally darted toward me. She too had the darkened marks on her face.

"Don't run from me," she ordered.

But it was too late. I knew what I needed to do to get her away from Thera.

I bounded the rest of the way up the stairs and ran in the opposite direction of her room. My lungs were burning, begging me to stop, but I forced my legs to continue.

I hadn't explored much of the other side of the house, but it didn't take long for Aris to find me.

The only warning I had was her crashing into the wall somewhere behind me.

It caused my heart to lodge in my throat and for a thrill to shoot up my spine. I knew it was dangerous to provoke her... but that didn't stop the excitement from filling me.

She had better self-control than the other demons, so maybe when she caught me—

A hard body hit my back, causing us both to tumble to the ground.

I let out a pained groan as her body weight pushed me into the ground. The carpet rubbed against my cheek and the exposed skin of my legs.

Her breath was hot against the back of my neck as the tip of her nose ran along the edge of my throat.

"I could have killed you," she growled, then hooked her hands under me and forced me to turn around to face her.

"Maybe you should," I countered.

Her eyes fell to my disheveled robe. Somewhere between my running for my life and our tussle, the tie had come loose and left most of my chest open to her. When her eyes trailed even further, we both realized how far up it had ridden, baring my pussy to her, the light panties she had stored for me doing nothing to conceal my need for her.

She let out another growl, and my cunt clenched and wetness pooled between my legs.

"I'm sorry I lied to you," I forced out. It was the last thing I wanted to talk about in that moment, but there was a small chance I would be able to get her attention like this again.

"Do you know how much money I spent on you?" she asked, her eyes trailing up my body to land on my erect nipple. With a delicate clawed hand, she pushed the robe fully out of the way.

"I said I'm sorry—"

"Will sorry bring back the money?" she continued, her voice hard. "Will sorry finish the job I brought you here to do?"

Her words caused my chest to ache.

"But I thought you wanted me to stay," I whispered. "I wanted to talk to you about it because maybe that's something I want too—"

Her mouth crashing against mine cut me off. Her tongue invaded my mouth, giving me no time to think. All I could do was respond, so I wrapped my arms around her, pulling her as close as she would allow.

Her hands gripped the robe, forcing it fully open while she trailed hot, open-mouthed kisses down my throat. I arched into her and grabbed her horns, pushing up so she would take a nipple into her mouth.

I moaned when she did and let my legs fall open for her, and she instantly took advantage of it, placing a hand between them, rubbing my damp underwear.

Her tongue circled one nipple before moving to the other one. She let her teeth graze against the sensitive flesh, and it pulled an embarrassingly loud whine from me.

A ripping sound filled the hallway, and cold air hit my aching pussy, but I couldn't find myself to care. Not when her fingers massaged my cunt, nor when she dipped two fingers inside me.

"Please, *please*," I begged, but if I was being truthful, I had no idea what I was begging for.

I unabashedly ground against her hand and used her horns to direct her to where I wanted her. She pumped her fingers in and out of me with little concern for hurting me. Something so different from what I was used to from her.

And I love it.

I loved the way her heel hit my clit with each powerful thrust. Loved the way she twisted and circled her fingers inside me.

And best of all, I loved when her teeth grazed every single part of my skin. It would only take one wrong move for her sharp teeth to nick me, but neither of us seemed to care in that moment. I was chasing my orgasm, and she was nothing but a very willing tool to help me get there.

I pushed her head down and hooked a leg over her shoulder. She followed my command, and in seconds her lips were circling my clit while her fingers still worked me.

"Harder," I commanded, tugging on her horns.

My breath was knocked out of me as her hand slammed into me. Delicious heat swirled in my belly.

"Yes, *Aris.* Just like that."

She gave my clit a hard suck, causing my back to bow.

"So good," I moaned. My orgasm was teasing me now. So close to rippling through my body yet so far.

Then she curled her fingers inside me and I cried out as the first wave hit me.

"Fuck yes, good. Good girl. Keep going."

My praise must have stirred something in her because, in a split second, it felt like all ties that had been holding her back snapped.

She fucked me harder and with no restraint. She lunged up, her mouth colliding with mine. Her tongue forced itself between my lips, the taste of my own wetness following.

I was stuck, writhing beneath her and unable to do a thing but take the fucking she was giving me.

When she pulled away, I met her hooded gaze.

"Don't make me leave," I whispered.

And then, just like that, the moment was gone.

Her eyes cleared, and her hand stopped. Her hair fell from her shoulder and tickled my cheek. I reached out, attempting to run my hand through it, but her hand shot forward to stop it.

Evidence of what had just happened between us was obvious on her fingers.

"Right," she muttered. "You need to leave soon. I'm sorry, I—"

The words got caught in her throat. Slowly, and oh so painfully, she stood.

She looked down at me with an expression I couldn't read.

"Clean yourself up and go back to my room," she ordered. "If you try to leave, I won't be there to save you."

And then she left me. Exposed, lying there on the ground like a used rag.

CHAPTER 19

ARIS

"I thought my work here was done," Yien said in a bored tone.

She leaned against the broken statue and looked up at the dull sky with a dazed expression.

I didn't have the energy to even roll my eyes at her attitude.

I had messed up... *again.* I hadn't planned to fuck her in the hallway like I had. My plan had been to let her stay in the house until I found a better way to get her passage home.

There were only a few ways one could get out of the Demon Realm. You either had the power to create a portal or you could find one.

And it had been years since the one in my realm had all but disappeared overnight.

I would have sent her home that same night, but I was one of the weakest of my kind and therefore would have to rely on my connections to get things done.

"I promised her I would get her home when her job was done," I said through gritted teeth.

I didn't *owe* Yien any kind of explanation, but I needed something to get her to help. I didn't want to have to lie to her, but I wasn't above it.

"And is it?" Yien asked. "She certainly took her time."

I bit my tongue.

Things had changed since I first brought Mia back to my realm.

I had grown attached to her in a way I never allowed myself to. Just her presence here had changed my life. Changed everything I had been focused on.

Cara was only a ghost of the past now. One that still haunted me, but ever since Mia... I found it didn't matter that much anymore. Not when I was focused on her instead.

To anyone else, it might seem like I had simply traded one human for another, but I knew it was more than that. I knew that anyone who met Mia and saw the fierceness that hid behind those eyes, they too would fall for her.

The moment in the hallway would serve as our goodbye.

It was a cold, callous goodbye. One that she didn't deserve. But it was the only one I could give.

If I let myself get close enough to her again to hear those cursed words from her lips, I truly might never let her go.

Don't make me leave.

The words swirled around my mind. A plea from her that sounded so utterly heartbreaking.

She doesn't belong here, I spat back at the voice. Images of my demon maid standing over her, ready to feast, hit me like a knife to the heart.

I am the reason she was in that situation to begin with.

And I wouldn't always be able to protect her. Not when she was but a human in his unforgiving realm.

"Yes," I spat. "Now can you get her back home or not?"

"Are you afraid Madam will take her from you if you go to her?" she asked, her eyes trailing to mine.

Her eyes were narrowed, and I swore I saw a slight smirk rest on her face. I didn't have time to think about how much her human seemed to have changed her as well. A being who once gave no indication of her feelings was almost *smirking* at me.

Yes, I wanted to say. If I ever so much as let Madam know that I was thinking of giving up this human, she would take her back in a heartbeat.

After all, to her, this human had great potential. A spirit seer or not, she could still see wraiths, something not every demon or human could manage. That alone would cause her to go up for auction again.

Or Madam herself might want to keep her.

I couldn't suppress my shiver at the thought.

The humans in the auction house looked frail, and their bones were often misshapen. I wasn't sure exactly what she or her customers had done to them, but I suspected it was far worse than what Mia experienced here.

"The auction house is no place for a human," I said.

She watched me for a moment before turning her attention back to the sky. Her shadows had gathered around us without me noticing. Some of them tickled my exposed skin.

"I know. I'm just trying to figure out why you seem so enamored with this human."

My hair stood on edge and my spine straightened. A low growl rumbled from my chest.

I couldn't help but be possessive of her. Yien was no threat—I knew that. But the way her lips twisted and her swirling shadows were enough for my instincts to go crazy.

"Don't act like you don't have your own companion waiting for you back in the Shadow Realm," I countered.

There was a long pause before she pushed herself off the statue and turned to me. For a moment, I thought she would refute my claim. It hadn't been that long since she carried word from her companion to mine, but things could change in an instant if us demons weren't careful.

"You're right, and I'd like to get back to her," she admitted. For some reason, that caused me to relax. Because if her human was still alive, that meant she was able to control herself around her. Probably better than I could around Mia.

"Show me where she is, and I'll have her back in the Human Realm before she knows it."

This is it.

Yien would go in there, send her back to her realm, and Mia would be gone from my life in the span of a few minutes.

You can still turn this around. Tell the shadow demon you changed your mind.

But I didn't allow myself to listen to those tempting thoughts.

They were the same ones that fantasized about keeping Mia here. About building a bigger, better house for her. About living a fulfilling, human-like life with her where we did nothing but spend our days together.

I had long since learned to shut those thoughts out, and I wouldn't allow them to control my actions.

I nodded, shielding my emotions, and motioned to the house, starting to walk back with heavy feet.

"She should be sleeping. Let me show you where."

CHAPTER 20

MIA

I had desperately tried to stay awake.

I knew something was going on with her. I tried to wait up to try and talk to her, but one hour turned to three and then six, and before I knew it, I had dozed off.

Panic woke me up.

Even in my sleep, I could feel the weight all around me. Suffocating me. There was something on me. Something I couldn't fight off.

I couldn't breathe. I couldn't move. I couldn't scream. No matter how many times I tried to gasp for air, I couldn't.

My eyes shot open, and I sat up, trying to see what was suffocating me in my sleep. At first, I thought it was another wraith coming for me, but then a shrill whine hit my ears.

I searched for the sound and met the bright green eyes of Momo. She was looking at me with narrowed eyes, her tail swaying around her. She was sitting on my chest, but surely *she* couldn't be the one making me feel like I couldn't breathe.

She's alive.

The last time I had seen her was when the demon who had

taken me had threatened to eat her right before chucking her across the room.

Relief hit me at the same time as a sinking realization.

But wait, if she is here...

My eyes darted around the dark room. My clock glowed in the dark, telling me it was three in the morning, moonlight shone through the small opening in the wall of my room, and the musky yet homey smell of my run-down apartment filled my senses.

I'm home. How the fuck—?

I jumped up, pushing the covers off, and Momo jumped to the floor. The world tilted, causing me to drop to my knees.

I'm home.

I couldn't tell how much time had passed, nor could I make heads or tails of how I had ended up back here.

It made everything else feel like a bad dream.

My chest twisted. *Was it a dream?* Had my guilt about scamming the townspeople snuck up on me and given me some hyper-realistic dreams?

Then panic set in. The world continued to spin. My breath caught in my chest.

It was real, right? Am I going insane?

No. It felt far too real to be a dream. I had been waiting for Aris. I was going to talk to her about staying. I remembered it vividly.

I remembered the smell of the house. The smell of *her* surrounding me as I cuddled underneath the blankets.

I let out a shuddered breath and turned to look at my room.

The small space could only hold a bed, a small dresser, and a closet. The rickety window was closed, but the wind outside could be heard pushing against it.

Besides that, it was silent, and I was back to the lonely life I had once lived.

It was real.

I gripped the robe I had stolen from Aris's closet. It was the only thing keeping me from spiraling. Because it didn't belong here. Because it still smelled like her.

It reminded me that everything that had happened in the Demon Realm had been *real*. That *Aris* was real.

But then how was I...

"Aris?" I called into the darkness. Cautiously at first, then when no one answered, I tried again, louder. "Aris!"

For a second, I thought that maybe she could be there with me. But there was no reaction from the darkness.

I pushed myself up and bounded down the steps and into the shop below. I stopped in my tracks when I took in the sight of it.

Not a single thing had changed.

Maybe there was a paper or two out of place, but it looked like I had never even left the place.

Another, smaller yet just as painful emotion filled me.

No one came to check on me.

I wasn't super good friends with anyone in the town, but I had been providing services to each and every one of them. None of them thought to come take a look?

I walked to the front, my bare feet slapping across the cold wooden floors.

Just outside my door was a pile of mail. Small for the time that I should have been gone.

Even the mailman didn't care about me.

I fell to the ground, my eyes fixated on the empty street outside. There was not a single soul out there.

Frustration, pain, and loneliness built up inside me.

I wanted to push open the doors. Scream at the top of my lungs. Beg for *anyone* to pay attention.

Though I knew inside that no one would come.

To them, I would just be another person, unable to deal with the harsh realities of this world.

Momo's high-pitched meow caused me to jump. She brushed across my side, causing my attention to turn to her.

With a small, sad smile, I picked her up and held her close to my chest.

"How did you survive without me?" I asked, knowing there was no way the food she had would have been enough.

She blinked up at me but didn't answer. Not that she could anyway.

"Was it the rats again?"

This time her head tilted to the side. I forced myself to let out a laugh, but it was short lived. I buried my face in her soft fur just as tears started to prick my eyes.

"It's just me and you, Momo."

CHAPTER 21

MIA

Three months later

"Pick anything you want," Agnus said with a sweet smile as she pulled me through the stalls in the farmers' market. "My treat!"

I gave her my best smile back. I hadn't planned on leaving the shop. After all, Sundays were one of my busiest days. People would filter in from the market, curiosity getting the better of them.

But of course, Agnus being my first customer all but took the rest of my day from me.

She visited me often to talk about her dead husband. So much sometimes that I barely got a word in before our session was up.

But she always left me a huge tip and a grateful smile.

She was actually one of the only repeat customers I had left.

Since coming back, I felt my need to lie to these people about their loved ones slipping. Just the night before, I had been searching the job boards, hoping to find something that would allow me to keep the shop but take fewer customers.

"You already pay me enough," I said.

She shook her head and pulled me up to a floral-smelling stall with all sorts of homemade lotions and soaps.

"Nonsense!" she said with a laugh. The old woman at the counter greeted her with a smile but eyed me warily. "It's the least I can do for all the help you've given me. Morning, Mags! Whatcha got for us?"

Mags paused for a moment before motioning to the far-right side of her table.

"Rose and honey soaps," she answered with far less enthusiasm than Agnus. The elderly woman might annoy me at times, but Mags's coldness toward her caused me to bristle.

"Oh, delightful!"

I smiled at Agnus as she picked up one and motioned for me to smell it. My eyes widened when the sweet floral scent filled my senses.

"Wait... That actually smells really nice!"

Mags let out a huff.

"I've been doing this for twenty years already," she answered. "*Of course* they smell good."

I bit my tongue and sent Agnus a smile.

"Well, if that's the case, I bet we're in good hands if we buy from her, huh?"

Agnus let out a laugh.

"We sure are! Three of these and my usual, please."

I stood silent as the ladies chatted while Mags gathered her stuff. They seemed friendly enough now that I had a chance to watch them. Maybe I had misjudged Mags.

"That bastard is still keeping her from me," Mags muttered under her breath. "I barely get calls anymore."

"Oh dear," Agnus said with a frown. "This all happened after your mom passed, didn't it?"

Mags nodded and handed over her bag with a sigh.

"Never mind," she said. "Twenty-eight, please."

I waited beside the stall while Agnus paid. When that was done, she looked at me, then turned back to Mags.

"Come visit Mia if you get a chance," she said. "I'm sure she can give you some answers about what's happening."

My jaw dropped.

"Agnus, you don't have to—"

"Shush now," she said and pulled me down the street. "She needs it more than most. Her husband divorced her and had been whispering some hateful things to her kid. They don't talk much anymore, and since her mom passed, she barely sees her."

I sent her a look.

"Must be difficult."

She nodded.

"Some people like her just need some... comfort," she explained. "Her mother was always against the marriage but *loved* Sofie, her daughter. They would visit her old house every Sunday after the farmers' market, but after she died they had to sell—"

"I didn't take you for much of a gossip, Agnus," I teased and threaded my arm in hers.

She threw her head back and let out a loud laugh, drawing some of the patrons' eyes.

"I'm doing this to help *you*, darling," she said. "Mags is a skeptic if I've ever seen one, so you better get your story straight before she comes to see you. Give her a week or two and she'll show, I promise."

I slowed my pace.

"What story?" I said with a nervous laugh.

Agnus rolled her eyes right before tugging me forward with a grip far stronger than someone her age should have.

"When I came to you, I was at my wits' end," she admitted, her suddenness taking me by surprise. "I believed. Wanted to believe so badly. But the moment you mentioned Bob's love for planes, I knew you were a fake."

We had moved out of the farmers' market and toward my shop, so thankfully no one could hear her declaration. So I stopped in my tracks, forcing her to face me. Her smile caused my heart to sink into my stomach.

"But for the first time in months, I was *happy*," she continued. "Truly, I was. So, I thought about it, then came back. But that time I came back for *you*."

I opened my mouth to speak, but no words came out.

"I know," she said with a laugh. "I probably shouldn't have blurted it out like that, but believe me when I say that I want to keep you in this town for as long as possible. So, my motives for recommending you and feeding you this information are entirely selfish."

I cleared my throat.

"But he had model planes everywhere," I muttered.

A twinkle lit her eyes.

"It was *compulsion*, not love," she explained. "If anything, he was terrified of them after crashing once."

I couldn't look her in the eyes. Instead, my gaze trailed to the shop. The sign was pitiful and needed to be redone. The steps were crumbling. The windows needed cleaning. The entire place looked awful.

What have I been doing the last three months?

"But I think you needed me too," she said, her hand coming to squeeze mine. This time I did look at her.

"I still do," I confessed, my voice cracking.

She shook her head.

"In recent months, I have seen a shift in you. You don't want to be here, in this town, anymore, and as much as I want to keep you... I should probably let you go."

I swallowed thickly and pulled the older woman into a hug.

"I won't be going anywhere anytime soon."

She let out a laugh.

"We will see, dear."

After three months of grieving my time in the Demon Realm, wishing for—no, not going there—for the first time I felt the need to change. To make something of my life here.

Because now I knew...

Aris wasn't coming back.

CHAPTER 22
ARIS

Fenix let out a loud sigh beside me as he sent out another burst of his power across the land.

The once graying, rocky soil was starting to turn a dark brown. The dead trees growing from it had straightened, and for the very first time, bright green leaves sprouted from their branches.

I patted the young demon on the head, trying my best to send him an encouraging smile.

"You can stop for today if it's too much," I said. "Let's go back home. I'm sure Thera has some broiled meat for us—"

A loud yell caused us both to turn and look toward the tree line. Just beyond was the house.

In the last three months, it had been renovated with the help of some of the weaker demons I took from the auction house.

I visited every week. I went there every time just to make sure the human I let go would remain free. It was hard to see others getting dragged to their deaths, but I would continue to do it just on the off chance that I would see her again.

The demons I collected had been in some of the auctions. Many separated from their families and sold for whatever Madam wanted. They were different from the ones that still lingered on the borders of my realm, digging up roots.

After Mia, I had realized just how lonely my existence was. It was another reason why I sought them out. I didn't expect them to stay or to even treat me the way they had, but all of them had surprised me by how well they acclimated.

They were scared at first. When I bought them, they thought the worst, but instead I gave them some projects and a few chores, and after they completed them, they were free to live in my realm so long as they heeded my rules.

1. No eating humans.

2. Respect each other.

3. Don't force anyone into anything.

4. Don't ruin others' work.

THERE HAD BEEN no incidents so far, and dare I say, some of them even started to feel like a sort of family unit. It had helped ease the loneliness.

Two things I never thought possible: to feel even more alone than before Mia, and to find a sort of family when I never had one.

I often looked forward to waking up now.

My demons took all the rotting wood out of the house and, with the help of those with the powers of plants or nature, rebuilt it. The fresh coat of yellow paint gleamed in the sunlight, and the patches of dark grass beneath it pulled the whole thing together.

Would she like it in yellow?

Another yell drew my attention to a smaller demon, who was now lying face first in the dirt. Taming animals was Shyla's job. I had tasked her with bringing in the weakest types of demons and spreading them out throughout the realm to assist in the growth of nature, but the role seemed to be too big for her.

One of the furry demons was sitting on top of her, its face barely visible save for two blood-red eyes. Its long, black tongue stuck out as it panted. Two more of its kind were sitting on either side of her, licking her hands.

"Get off me!"

Fenix let out a laugh, and I couldn't help the tilt of my lips at the sound of it.

"Go help her," I ordered.

He shook his head and pushed himself off the ground to run to her.

With ease, he moved the one sitting on her and helped her into a standing position. She looked like she might cry.

I opened my mouth to speak, but Thera's yell from the house stopped me.

"The meal is ready! Hurry before the blood thickens!"

The two younger demons bounded inside. I let myself follow them slowly, enjoying the moment of peace we had.

I couldn't remember a time my realm had been so lively. It was called the Deadlands for a reason. But now, there was grass growing and trees that could even bear fruit someday.

Would the green and the fruit make her more comfortable here?

The mist that had settled over the area was still there, though much lighter than before, and hopefully with a few more demons we could get rid of it once and for all.

My stomach turned, and a sour feeling spread across my tongue.

It was coming along so nicely... Yet there would always be something—someone—missing.

I had tried so hard not to think about Mia—*the human*—since I had Yien sneak into our room while she slept and send her away.

But her smell still lingered in my bed, on my clothes, and in parts of the house that remained untouched by anyone else.

I had the chance to get rid of the smell, but every time the thought crossed my mind... I found myself unable to.

As much as I tried to distance myself, every part of my life was still very much intertwined with her. And I found myself often wishing I had never asked Yien to take her away from me.

I went back to the auction house for her. I rebuilt my house for her. The entire realm was changing only so I might be able to bring her back home if I ever saw her again.

Can a human survive here? she had asked when she caught sight of my house.

Probably not then, but maybe one could now.

"Aris?" Thera called, her head poking out of one of the first-floor windows. She met me with a smile as if I had not broken her leg for touching my human three months ago. "Come, everyone's starting without you!"

I gave her a forced smile.

"Coming."

Yes... this is my life now.

One I should be grateful for.

One that absolutely did not need the human in it.

Right?

CHAPTER 23
MIA

I looked up at my shop's new sign with a heavy feeling.

It looked great.

I had spent the last month redoing the shop with all the savings I had managed.

Agnus had kept her promise and began spreading the word about my services. Mags came in not long after she predicted, and, thanks to the knowledge she shared, Mags too became a regular.

I should have felt bad about using the gossip Agnus fed me to reel in customers, but it had helped put food on the table and take my mind away from other things.

And Agnus seemed to be having a hell of a time. She no longer came in for my services. Instead, we just made some tea and had snacks together while gossiping.

She was my only friend in this town, and one that I treasured dearly.

But still... Nothing seemed to matter.

The memories of the Demon Realm never left me. While it had been a frightening experience, I had tried many times to recreate the steps I had taken the night the red-winged demon had visited me, but it never worked. She never showed up again.

I knew I should have moved on, but it was like I was incapable of it. It didn't matter that she and I were from different worlds. Or that I hadn't wanted to be there in the first place.

Every night I dreamt of Aris, and when I woke up, I swore I could still feel the brush of her skin against mine. The memory of her was ingrained in me, and I couldn't forget the feeling of her lips against mine.

It was all a constant reminder of what I was missing. What I had lost.

I should have told her the truth earlier. I should have told her I wanted to stay. I shouldn't have let her push me away.

I sat on my desk, drinking a bottle of the cheapest rosé I could find.

I didn't know what I was going to do. Would the rest of my life be like this? A constant cycle of desperately missing the demon who had bought me and almost killed me while scamming the small town of their money?

When I was younger, I used to think that I would accomplish something special with the time I had here... Yet there I was, getting drunk by myself and dreaming about being whisked away into some far-off, lifeless realm. Again.

I almost didn't believe it when a shimmering portal opened in front of me. I thought I was hallucinating or flat out drunk when the familiar leather wings poked out, followed by a glimpse of stark white hair.

But I sure as hell started to believe it was real when the portal closed behind her, and she met my gaze with a wicked grin.

I chucked the wine bottle at her head and scrambled over my desk, trying to get away. The sound of the bottle landing on the wood floor should have warned me, but I wasn't prepared for the demon to appear right in front of me.

"Looks like Aris has been *naughty*," she said with a laugh. I jerked back. Her clawed hand gripped my shirt and forced me close to her face.

"Letting a human go isn't against the rules," I replied, though I had no idea if it was true or not.

Her lips twisted into a smile that caused my blood to run cold.

"No," she admitted. "But she's been getting on my nerves, so I have come to... rectify the issue."

I raised a brow at her, trying to hide the fact that the mention of Aris's name was doing things to my heart.

"I have come to make a deal with you."

I shook my head. "You fucking kidnapped me last time. Why the hell would I make any kind of deal with you?"

She inhaled deeply. "Your fear smells so good. No wonder you grew on her."

"Stop smelling me," I spat out.

She let go of my shirt to stand back with her hands on her hips.

"Come back with me, and I will let Aris purchase you again," she offered. "I kept hoping she would buy another human, but instead she's buying all the pitifully weak demons, and it's messing with my sales. I'm sure once she sees you again, she'll leave us alone for good."

Wait.

I can... go back?

"And what do I get out of this?" I asked.

It was her turn to raise a brow.

"Going back to Aris isn't enough?"

My chest puffed. "Why would I want to go back there? I have a good life here."

Her silence spoke louder than anything she could have said. Of course I had been waiting for this opportunity, but now that it was here... Could I really take it? Could I really leave the human world for good?

Will Aris still want me?

"Take it or leave it," she spat. "My auction starts in less than five minutes, and I won't be coming back."

I swallowed thickly.

"Can I... prepare first?"

She shrugged. "If you can do it in... three minutes."

My mind was made up. I had imagined this enough times to know exactly what I needed to do.

I packed a bag of clothes and underwear and whatever else I could fit in there. Then I left the shop door unlocked, filled Momo's bowls and petted her, and finally, I left a note for Agnus.

Thank you for everything. I will miss you.

Please take care of Momo.

The demon sighed as I placed the note on the desk, right where Agnus wouldn't miss it in the morning.

"Come on," she growled and pulled me backwards into the portal.

CHAPTER 24

ARIS

This would be my last auction. It had to be. I couldn't take it anymore.

The house was growing far too much, and I just had to face it... Mia was gone for good.

I sat down in the back in my usual seat and waited for the auction to start.

I had forced myself to come later this time, in hopes that I could get here right as it started. It was unheard of, but today they seemed to be running late.

Murmurs broke out among the demons, and some even got visibly upset.

"Bring them out!" one of them growled from the right, standing up.

A few others laughed at him.

"Don't get too excited now," another teased.

He huffed and settled into his seat.

My eyes were focused on the curtain that hid the stage. I couldn't hear anything behind it.

But then, out of nowhere, it was pulled back. Everyone sat up in their seats, ready to get a glimpse of the humans, but we were met with an empty stage.

Confused whispers spread throughout the room, until our host, Madam, stepped through a portal.

"Sorry to have kept you waiting," she said with a dangerous-looking smile. "But I have brought a special gift."

Her hand was still in the portal, so we couldn't see what she was holding. But as soon as a familiar head with brown hair and hazel eyes appeared, my breath caught in my throat.

It can't be true. Can it? What kind of coincidence is this? On the very last auction I was planning to attend?

Did Madam go back and get her? How could she be taken from her home again? Anger lit my veins on fire.

"Mia, a spirit seer and our first item," she announced as she pulled Mia out abruptly, causing her to glare at Madam.

She was dressed in a sweater and jeans, and this time she had a backpack with her.

She prepared to come. She wasn't kidnapped this time.

That knowledge caused hope to burst inside me and excitement to shoot up my spine.

Mia had willingly come to the Demon Realm. For... me?

"This is her second time in the auction, and therefore, we are raising her price," Madam said. "Last time, she sold for seventy thousand. Let's start with a hundred."

There was silence. Not many people could afford that, and anything was rarely sold for that much here.

When Madam's eyes met mine, I knew.

She wanted me to spend all my money on her. Normally, I wouldn't want to play her game, but this time I didn't care. For Mia, I would play whatever game she wanted.

A hand raised.

"Do I hear one-ten?"

Another hand raised.

"I see one-thirty."

It was my hand that raised this time.

"You brought her for me," I said, letting my voice carry across the room.

"Only if you can pay."

I let out a growl. Of course I could pay. We both knew I had money to spare.

"Oh, is that one-forty?" Another hand rose.

I let out a curse and pushed myself to my feet. "Two hundred thousand!"

Madam threw her head back and laughed.

"She's all yours, Aris of the Deadlands."

This was a surreal moment, one I had dreamed about but never thought would come.

I let my legs take me to the stage, not taking my eyes off Mia the entire time.

She is here. She is truly here.

By the time I reached the stage, reality had sunk in.

I held my hand out for Mia to take.

Her eyes were wide, and she looked at me as if she too couldn't believe what was happening.

"Oh, and Aris?" Madam called. "You're banned from the auction."

I turned to her but was met with a bright light.

"Fuck." I pulled Mia to me, holding her as close as I could without crushing her.

Moving through the portal caused my stomach to flip, but before I knew it, the light was gone, and instead of the auction house, I was in my own realm.

Mia pushed me away so she could look up at me. A frown

pulled at her lips. She was mad at me, and I would take it because she was here.

"You sent me back."

I nodded stiffly.

"I thought you'd be better with your own kind," I said. "I didn't want to. I wanted to keep you so badly, but I knew I was being selfish."

Her hands gripped my robe.

"I wanted to stay," she whispered. "I tried to go back to normal, but I kept thinking about you. It's so stupid because I was living a good life in the Human Realm but as soon as she came to me and offered to bring me back, I just left with her, and I—"

I swooped in to cover her mouth with my own. She met my kiss back with an eagerness that caused my head to swim. I pulled away just as her tongue darted out.

"I'm sorry," I breathed.

"You should be," she said. "I don't fully understand how this is going to work, but I want it to."

I sent her a smile.

"It will," I assured her and motioned for her to look at the house. "I made sure of that."

Her eyes widened when she took in the new house.

"You remodeled?"

"And got some help," I said. "There's a few people I want you to meet, but that can come later, for tonight I want you—"

She tugged me down to crash her lips to mine. This time, I didn't try to stop her as she explored my mouth. My hands gripped her tight, and I forced her legs around my waist while I carried her into the house.

"Don't you dare send me away again," she breathed against my mouth.

"Never."

THANK you for reading TAKEN TO THE DEADLANDS! If you were curious about what happened to the other humans at the auction you can find out in TAKEN TO THE SHADOW REALM!

My whole life I had been groomed to be the *perfect wife*, knowing one day I would be sold off to create an even more *perfect heir*.

And then I was kidnapped.

Taken away to a fantasy land where a cold yet sensitive shadow demon decided to buy me as her companion.

Was it wrong that I was happy to finally *be free?*

Or that I started to feel things for the cold demon?

Either way, I would enjoy my freedom, and maybe if I was lucky I could convince my new master to make use of her *purchase.*

WANT to be in the know? Join my newsletter for publishing updates and free shorts!

JOIN my Patreon and you will get access to all stories BEFORE they are published.

If you join now you will get free stories and deleted chapters!

There is also a tier for NSFW art that is exclusive for my Patreon members

Check it out here or go to https://www.patreon.com/ellemae books

127

IF YOU LIKED THIS, PLEASE REVIEW!

Reviews really help indie authors get their books out there so, please make sure to share your thoughts!

About the Author

Elle is a native Californian who has lived in Los Angeles for most of her life. From the very start, she has been in love with all things fantasy and reading. As soon as Elle found out that writing books could be a career, she picked up a pen and paper. While the first ones were about scorned love and missed opportunities of lunchtime love, she has grown to love the fantasy genre and looks forward to making a difference in the world with her stories.

Loved this book? Please leave a review!

For more behind the scene content, check out my Patreon!

X   x.com/mae_books

instagram.com/ellemaebooks

goodreads.com/ellemae

patreon.com/ellemaebooks

tiktok.com/@ellemaebooks